Joe and Samantha saw someone coming over.

Joe realized that it was Timmy. The boy wasn't smiling—far from it, in fact. He looked worried about something.

"Hi," said Joe.

"What's up?" Samantha asked.

Timmy frowned. "I don't know how to say this, but . . . well, you remember the trophies I showed you the other day?"

"Sure," said Joe.

"Remember the big one?" Timmy continued. "The one with my grandfather's name on it?"

"Of course," said Sam. "What about it?"

Timmy swallowed hard. "It's gone."

Other books in the
WISHBONE™ Mysteries series:

WISHBONE Mysteries

THE STOLEN TROPHY

by Michael Jan Friedman

WISHBONE™ created by Rick Duffield

Big Red Chair Books™, *A Division of Lyrick Publishing*™

This book is a work of fiction. The characters, incidents, and dialogues are products of the author's imagination and are not to be construed as real. Any resemblance to actual events or persons, living or dead, is entirely coincidental.

 Big Red Chair Books™, *A Division of Lyrick Publishing*™
300 E. Bethany Drive, Allen, Texas 75002

©1998 Big Feats! Entertainment

Edited by Kevin Ryan

Copy edited by Jonathon Brodman

Cover concept and design by Lyle Miller

Interior illustrations by Don Adair

Wishbone photograph by Carol Kaelson

Library of Congress Catalog Card Number: 97-74832

ISBN: 1-57064-485-3

First printing: February 1998

10 9 8 7 6 5 4 3 2 1

For Whitey Ford,
Mammal of Mystery

FROM THE BIG RED CHAIR . . .

Oh . . . hi! Wishbone here. You caught me right in the middle of some of my favorite things—books. Let me welcome you to the WISHBONE MYSTERIES. In each story, I help my human friends solve a puzzling mystery. In *THE STOLEN TROPHY*, my best friend, Joe Talbot, and I investigate a mystery involving a valuable basketball trophy that ends up missing.

The story takes place late in the fall, during the same time period as the events you'll see in the second season of my WISHBONE television show. In this story, Joe is fourteen, and he and his friends are in the eighth grade. Like me, they are always ready for adventure . . . and a good mystery.

You're in for a real treat, so pull up a chair and a snack and sink your teeth into *THE STOLEN TROPHY*.

Chapter One

Wishbone, a small white terrier with one brown ear, paced back and forth on the leaf-littered grass next to the asphalt basketball court outside Sequoyah Middle School.

"Come on, Joe!" he cheered. "Take the ball to the hoop!"

Joe was the lean, athletic kid with short, dark hair who happened to be Wishbone's best friend. He was also the boy with whom Joe lived.

At the moment, Joe was dribbling a basketball through a crowd of defenders, smoothly working his way to his opponents' basket.

Dribbling first with his right hand and then with his left, Joe avoided one last defender and laid the ball up against the fiberglass backboard. A moment later, the ball sank neatly through the hoop.

"Way to go!" said Wishbone, his tail wagging furiously.

"That's two!" cried David, one of Joe's two best human friends. He was referring to the number of points Joe had scored when he made the basket.

David was the kind of kid who loved to invent all sorts of things. But even on his best day, he couldn't have invented a nicer play than the one Joe had just pulled off.

"Looks like we're ahead now," Samantha said good-naturedly.

Sam was Joe's other best friend. She had blond hair—tied back in a ponytail at the moment—and one of the nicest smiles Wishbone had ever seen. As long as Wishbone had known Sam, he had never heard her say a bad word about anyone.

"Wait a minute," said Damont Jones, waving both arms back and forth. "That's not a basket. Joe double-dribbled."

"You're out of your mind," David responded. "That play was clean as a whistle, Damont."

"Yeah," Wishbone echoed, "clean as a really *clean* whistle."

Damont was the opportunist of the group, always looking for a way to make himself come out on top. That was true of everything the kid took part in—not just basketball.

But when Damont looked around, he could see his teammates weren't giving his argument any support. Disgusted, he gave up.

After one team scored a basket, the other one was supposed to take the ball out of bounds and pass it back in. With that in mind, Damont snatched up the ball, stepped behind the out-of-bounds line, and looked for a teammate to toss to. Colby, a big kid with a dark-haired crew cut, came over quickly to catch the pass.

As soon as Damont came back onto the court, Colby passed the ball back to him. Then Damont put on a burst of speed and dribbled the basketball across the midcourt line.

Two of Damont's teammates were racing ahead of him along the sidelines, each of them looking for a pass so he could cut to the basket. However, they were guarded by Samantha and David.

Normally, Wishbone was a law-abiding dog. But when Joe and his friends were playing defense, he had only one thing on his mind.

"Steal the ball!" he cheered. "Take it away!"

Damont could have tried to pass the ball to one of his teammates. But, being Damont, he preferred to score all his team's points by himself. So he lowered his head, bounced the ball from his left hand to his right, and drove toward the basket in his fancy white-and-gold sneakers.

Damont was a pretty good athlete—though he wasn't nearly as good as he gave himself credit for. Besides, Joe was ready for him, perfectly balanced on the balls of his feet.

As Damont went by, Joe shuffled sideways to his left and knocked the basketball away from

Damont. Then, grabbing the ball and dribbling as fast as he could, Joe sped downcourt in the opposite direction.

Wishbone leaped high in the air and did a backward flip. "Way to go!" he said approvingly.

Basketball was one of his favorite sports. He enjoyed the excitement of the game, the fast pace, and the suspense of not knowing what would happen next. He loved watching a nice pass, a skillful dribble, or a successful long-range shot.

But when it came to sheer thrills and chills, there was nothing like a good steal to get Wishbone's heart pumping. It was fun to watch someone track the ball handler, wait patiently for his chance, then snatch the basketball away—just as Joe had snatched it from Damont.

At that point, Joe had only two players to beat—the two tallest kids on Damont's team. One by one, they tried to steal the ball back. But Joe dribbled circles around them and stayed on course.

"'Atta boy!" said Wishbone. "Lay it in, Joe!"

A moment later, Joe did just that. With no one on Damont's team left to stop him, he made an easy layup. The ball rolled around the rim of the basket, then went in for two points.

"Fourteen to eleven!" David cried out, keeping score. "One more basket and we win!"

"Ya gotta love it!" Wishbone chimed in.

After that, the ball went up and down the court a few times, though no one scored. Eventually, it wound up in the hands of a boy on Joe's team—a slim, blond fellow named Wade.

Normally, Wishbone knew, Wade was very careful to protect the ball. This time, however, he was too busy worrying about the kid guarding him to see Damont sneaking up from behind.

Joe saw what was happening and called out a warning. But by then, it was too late. Damont had already hooked the basketball away from Wade and was dribbling away with it.

It looked to Wishbone as if Damont had smacked Wade's arm aside in the process. But that didn't stop Damont.

He hurtled downcourt, all alone. But instead of going for a layup, Damont pulled up at the three-point line and launched what the kids called a "bomb." It went up high in the air and came down right into the hoop.

Swish! Damont's team had tied up the score. Now either team could win by scoring a single basket.

Wishbone enjoyed the drama of it all. So did most of the other kids, judging by their expressions.

But Wade didn't seem to like it at all. The boy was red-faced. He looked embarrassed to have lost the basketball to Damont—especially when Damont might have gotten the ball illegally.

"Wait a minute," he said. "Damont fouled me."

"I did not," Damont replied. For emphasis, he

put on the most skeptical expression he could muster.

"You sure did," Wade argued.

"Did not," Damont insisted.

"Did," the other boy insisted even louder.

Joe put his hand on Wade's shoulder. "Hey, what's the big deal? Let's forget it, okay?"

Wade scowled. "I don't want to forget it. That Damont always gets his way. Someday, somebody's going to get even with him."

Suddenly, Wishbone heard the sound of a car approaching. Turning, he caught sight of a white station wagon. It slowed down and pulled up at the curb nearest the basketball court.

Anthony's mom was at the wheel. Her son was one of the better rebounders on Joe's team.

"Anthony," she called. "It's time."

Joe looked at Anthony. "Time?" he echoed.

Anthony slapped his forehead with the heel of his hand. "For my Wednesday orthodontist appointment. I forgot."

"Say good-bye to your friends and let's go," said his mother. "I don't want to be late again."

Anthony looked helpless. "Sorry," he said, looking around at Joe and his other teammates.

Then he got into the station wagon with his mother. A moment later, they drove off down the leaf-covered street.

Damont grinned as he picked up the ball. "Hey, Joe, that's too bad. Without Anthony, you've only got four players." He shrugged. "I guess you'll have to forfeit the game."

"Don't look so happy about it," said Samantha.

Normally, she could forgive anybody—even Damont—for anything. But, obviously, she wasn't in the mood for Damont's shenanigans.

"Me . . . happy?" Damont replied. He dribbled the ball between his legs, and his smile widened. "Whatever gave you that idea?"

"Oh, I don't know," said David. "I'd say that big ol' grin on your face could be a clue."

All the kids looked at one another. None of them seemed to have a solution to the problem of Anthony's departure.

Maybe David could have invented a machine to play basketball with them, if he was given enough time. Unfortunately, they needed another player right then and there.

"Too bad," said Wishbone. He didn't know what was worse—the game being decided by forfeit, or Damont getting his way.

Just then, Samantha pointed to something behind Wishbone. "Wait a minute," she said. "Maybe we don't have to forfeit after all."

The terrier turned and followed Sam's gesture. He saw a youngster about the same age as Joe and his friends standing near the school building, his hands stuck deep in his pockets.

"I would have noticed him earlier," Wishbone said, "except the wind was blowing in the wrong direction." After all, he *did* have the best sense of smell of any dog in town.

"Timmy?" said David.

The boy came closer. He had bright orange hair and a face full of big, brown freckles.

"Hi, David," he said.

David turned to Joe. "This is Timmy Ashbury, the new kid in my class who I was telling you about."

He lowered his voice to little more than a whisper—but not so much that Wishbone couldn't hear it. The terrier's sense of hearing was almost as good as his sense of smell.

"I've seen Timmy play," David told Joe. "He's pretty good."

Joe thought for a moment. "Well," he said at last, "it's not like we've got much of a choice."

He went over to the newcomer and put his hand out. "My name's Joe."

The red-haired kid shook Joe's hand. "Mine's Timmy."

"Listen," said Samantha, "would you like to play some basketball, Timmy? We've got a tie game, and we just lost a player."

Timmy looked around at Joe and his friends. "Er . . . sure, why not?"

"Good," said Joe. "Come on, it's our ball."

Samantha picked up the ball and stepped behind the out-of-bounds line. Then she tossed the ball to David, who passed it to Timmy. As Joe and Wade shot up the sidelines, Timmy dribbled the ball up the court.

It seemed to Wishbone that Timmy was a pretty good ball handler. "Almost as good as Joe," he said, "and that's saying a lot."

Unfortunately, Damont was the one covering Timmy. Joe and his friends had learned what to expect from Damont, but Timmy was new in town. He didn't know what kind of tricks Damont might play.

Damont didn't wait long to take advantage of that fact.

"Hey, new kid," he said tauntingly. "Why don't you try and dribble past me? I'll bet you're too slow."

Wishbone could see by Timmy's expression that he didn't like being made fun of. But then, no one did.

Still, Timmy held on to his concentration. He continued to dribble the ball, keeping it away from Damont as he looked for an open teammate.

Damont snickered. "Come on, new kid. Show us how good you are. Go ahead and blow by me."

Wishbone wagged his tail in anticipation. He would have liked nothing better than to see Timmy run circles around Damont. But if he knew Damont— and he did—the boy had a trick up his sleeve.

"Don't listen to him," Joe called, trying to get free for a pass. "Play your game, Timmy. Don't let him rush you."

"That's right," said Damont. "Don't let me rush you, new kid. Take all day if you need to."

Finally, Damont's remarks had the desired effect. Gritting his teeth, Timmy crossed over from his left hand to his right hand and darted forward.

But when Damont tried to stop him, he didn't move fast enough. It looked as though Timmy was going to go right by him, after all. And if he did, he had a pretty clear shot at the basket.

Wishbone leaped up on his hind legs. "This could be it!" he said. "If Timmy scores, the game's over!"

And it would be Damont's fault that his team had lost. If Damont hadn't teased Timmy, the new boy might not have been tempted to dribble past him. Once again, it looked as if one of Damont's schemes had backfired on him.

But as Timmy went by, Damont took a giant step and brought his foot down on the back of the new boy's sneaker. The next thing anyone knew, Timmy's sneaker was flying through the air and he was hopping around on his other foot. He watched helplessly as the ball bounced away from him.

"Yikes!" said Wishbone. "What a dirty trick *that* was!"

But Damont wasn't finished. As he went for the ball, the Damonster plowed right into Timmy's shoulder.

It was hard enough to hop around on only one foot. When somebody bumped you as well,

it became downright impossible. With a yelp, Timmy hit the hard surface of the playground.

As it turned out, Damont didn't get the ball—but one of his teammates did. As Colby dribbled it the other way, Joe's team hurried back on defense—all except Timmy, of course. He was still lying on the ground.

"Time out!" called Wade. "Timmy's hurt!"

"That's not our problem!" Damont replied. He jumped in front of Colby. "Give me the ball!"

Startled, Colby passed it to him. Dribbling the ball as fast as he could, Damont zigged and zagged back and forth across the court. He ignored the cries of his teammates as he outmaneuvered one of Joe's teammates after the other.

Finally, he saw an opening and drove to the basket. But just as he let a shot go, Joe came out of nowhere and blocked it. Before anyone else could grab the basketball, it went out of bounds.

"Our ball!" cried Damont. "It went out off Joe!"

"Hold on!" said Joe. "What about Timmy?"

"What about him?" asked Damont.

Joe looked over his shoulder. "He's hurt."

Timmy came walking over. Despite a scraped knee and a little limp from his spill, he had a determined look on his face.

"I'm not hurt," the boy said. "I'm okay. I just got the wind knocked out of me for a second."

"What are you talking about?" asked Wade. "Damont gave you a flat tire—and then he banged into you!"

"It was an accident!" said Damont.

"Was not!" Wade replied. "Come on, Damont, I *saw* you!"

"It's all right," said Timmy. "I mean it. Let's just play."

"You sure?" asked Joe.

Timmy looked at Damont for a moment, his features still locked in a mask of determination. Then he nodded.

"I'm sure, Joe. I mean, the game's almost over, right? It'd be a shame to stop now."

Wishbone tilted his head. "The kid's being a good sport about it, all right. Not everybody would have taken what Damont did in stride."

Ryan, one of the other players on Damont's team, took the ball out of bounds and passed it to Colby. The game was on again.

Suddenly, Wishbone felt a big, wet drop fall on his face. He looked up and saw a row of big, dark-bellied clouds coming toward him from the horizon. Then the terrier felt a second drop and a third.

"Uh-oh," said Samantha. "It's starting to rain."

"Play through it!" Joe shouted. "We can still get the rest of the game in. Just keep going."

It seemed like a possibility, too—for a second or two, anyway. Then the big, fat drops began to come down harder and quicker.

"Man," said David, "we've got to get inside. It's really starting to come down now."

"Let's go to my house," said Timmy. "I've got a basement full of cool stuff. We can hang out there till the rain stops."

With that, he began to run down the street. Joe, Samantha, and David looked at one another for a moment. Then Joe shrugged and all the other kids followed—even Damont, who had tucked the ball under his arm.

Wishbone was the last to get going. But then, he liked the rain.

To him, a November storm—like this one— always smelled of excitement and adventure and faraway places. The only thing he *didn't* like about it was that it sometimes ruined a basketball game or two.

"Oh, well," he said.

Wagging his tail, Wishbone scampered after the kids on all four legs. Being naturally curious, he was already wondering what kind of cool stuff Timmy might have stashed away in that basement.

Chapter Two

Joe looked back to make sure Wishbone was coming along. Then he ran after Timmy a little faster, heavy drops of rain plunking on his head and shoulders with increasing regularity.

Joe didn't really mind that the basketball game had been interrupted by the rain. With victory depending on the next basket, the situation had gotten a little tense. Mostly, it was *Damont* who had gotten tense. But then, it wasn't the first time Damont had taken the idea of winning a little too seriously.

As Joe and his friends followed, Timmy ran across a lawn to a white house with black shutters. When Timmy reached the front door, he swung it wide open for the others.

The kids all made their way inside. Wishbone came in last of all.

He seemed to hesitate for a moment. Then, as

if his instincts had won out over his manners, he shook himself dry.

Seeing what Wishbone was doing, Joe apologized to Timmy.

But Timmy just laughed. "It's okay," their host said. "It's only water."

Then, as if on cue, the sky opened up and the rain began to come down in heavy, windswept sheets.

"Made it in the nick of time," said David.

"You can say that again," Samantha replied.

"Okay," said David. "Made it in the nick—"

But he couldn't finish his remark this time. Sam had good-naturedly clamped her hand over his mouth to stop him.

"We get the idea," she told him.

"Come on," said Timmy. "The basement is this way."

He led the kids along a short hallway into the kitchen, where there were a whole lot of copper pots and pans on one wall. Timmy opened a door leading off from the kitchen and went down a flight of stairs.

Joe followed him down. So did all the others, including Wishbone. They found themselves in a big, wood-paneled room.

As it turned out, Timmy hadn't kidded them one bit. His basement really *was* full of cool stuff.

In one corner, there was an old-fashioned barber chair on a thick, metal pedestal. Its red-leather upholstery was all shiny and new-looking despite its age. The chair's wrought-iron footrest displayed the name of its manufacturer in fancy letters.

"'Kepler,'" said Samantha. "Hey, that's my name."

"Maybe your family used to make barber chairs," David suggested.

She shrugged. "I didn't think so. I guess I'll have to ask my dad."

In another corner stood a big, old wooden display cabinet with thick glass windows. It was full of knickknacks—too many for Joe to count.

His eye was drawn to a couple of toy airplanes made out of tin. The planes were blue-and-red, with propellers instead of jet engines. Their pilots were blond men with goggles and handlebar moustaches.

"Look at these," said Samantha, as she pointed to a pair of metal salt-and-pepper shakers. Each one had a little set of legs like a piece of furniture.

Sam laughed. "They're adorable."

Wade liked a metal serving tray with the name of a soft-drink company on it. It had a picture of a little kid in his best clothes drinking soda pop from a bottle.

There were lots of other items in the display cabinet. Joe could have looked at them for a long time. He would have, too, except there were many other things to check out in Timmy's basement.

Joe walked over to an assortment of sporting equipment leaning against one wall. He saw a set of ancient golf clubs, a trio of beat-up wooden baseball bats, and a well-used hockey stick.

There were also a couple of old-style tennis rackets. Their faces were small compared to the kind of rackets used today, Joe thought. They weren't constructed of fiberglass or graphite, either. They were made completely of wood that had been painted.

David picked up one racket. It had a wooden frame surrounding its face that was held together with screws.

"What's this for?" he asked Timmy.

"So the wood won't warp," the boy explained. "Anyway, that's what my dad told me. But it was *his* dad who used to play with the rackets."

The tennis rackets were interesting, all right. Wishbone must have thought so, too, judging by the way he was staring at them. But Joe's attention had been drawn to a wooden shelf built into the far wall.

It had five trophies on it. All of them were old, with tall metal figures and marble bases. The oldest and biggest one by far was to the left. It had a big statue of a basketball player taking an old-fashioned set shot—which was like a jump shot without the jump.

The trophy had a metal plaque with an inscription on its base. Joe read the inscription out loud.

"'Kingsport Cougars, Appalachian League Champions, 1943. Lionel Beatty, Guard.'" He smiled. "Wow!"

"'Wow!' is right," Samantha commented.

By then, the other kids had gathered around Joe. They leaned forward and squinted to read the plaque, too.

"Who's Lionel Beatty?" asked Damont, his basketball still tucked securely under his arm.

"That was my grandfather," Timmy explained.

Damont looked at him with doubt. "Really?"

Timmy nodded. "My mom's father."

"And your dad's father played tennis," David noted. "You had athletes on both sides of your family."

"That's right," said Timmy. "That's why *I'm* a good athlete."

Damont grunted. "You're not *that* good."

"Yes, he *is*," Wade said. "Leave him alone, Damont. I think Timmy's had enough of the 'new kid' routine for one day."

Damont looked as if he was going to say something to Wade, but he didn't. He just frowned.

Timmy used a sweeping hand gesture to indicate the entire contents of his basement. "Everything here came from someone in my family. My mom and dad have kept it all in good shape so I can have it when I grow up."

"Cool," said Samantha.

"I'll bet this stuff is worth a lot of money," said David.

"Definitely," Timmy replied.

He went over to the display cabinet, opened a drawer, and took out a printed card. He handed it to David.

"This is the card of the antiques dealer in town," Timmy explained.

"Sure," said Joe, looking over David's shoulder. "Oakdale Attic Antiques. It's between the bank and the movie theater."

"I guess so," Timmy replied. "Anyway, they've offered to buy all of our stuff, everything included."

"Are you going to sell it?" asked Colby.

"No way," said Timmy. "My parents would never let go of any of it. They're too nostalgic about it to sell it at *any* price."

"That's crazy," Damont remarked. "Why keep something when you can turn it in for cold, hard cash?"

David rolled his eyes. "I could've predicted Damont would say something like that."

Damont eyed him. "What's *that* supposed to mean?"

"This stuff is worth more than money," Samantha explained. "It's like a photo album that goes way back. It lets Timmy see what the people in his family used to work with and play with."

"Almost like a time machine," David added.

Sam nodded. "Almost."

Wishbone barked as if he agreed. The kids laughed.

"Can I hold your grandfather's trophy?" asked Colby.

Timmy sighed. "Will you be careful with it?"

"I'll be *real* careful," Colby promised.

"Okay," said Timmy.

Colby reached over and picked it up off the shelf. "It's heavy," he said, "isn't it?"

"A lot heavier than the trophies they make today," Timmy agreed. "That's because it's made of metal and marble, not plastic."

Up close, the old trophy looked even cooler. "Can I hold it, too?" Joe asked hopefully.

"Sure," said Timmy.

Colby handed it to Joe. *It really* is *heavy*, Joe thought. He handled it carefully, turning it around in his hands and examining it from every angle. It was unusual.

"You know," said Damont, "it's getting really stuffy down here. I'm going to open a window."

He put his ball down and pulled a folding chair over to the only window in the whole basement. Then he got on the chair and unlatched the window lock. After he had done that, he swung the window open.

Immediately, Joe felt a breeze on his face. He smelled its freshness. He also heard the pattering of the rain striking the open window.

Joe hadn't realized it until then, but it really *had* been stuffy in Timmy's basement. For once, Damont had had a good idea.

Wishbone must have thought so, too. His tail was wagging.

Joe returned the trophy to Timmy. "Here," he said. "I don't want to break it or anything."

As Joe watched, Timmy placed the trophy back on the shelf. Then he brushed his hands off.

By then, the rain had begun to let up. Joe could hear a bird chirping outside through the open window. He thought he could even see a ray of sunshine in Timmy's backyard.

"Looks like the rain's almost over," Joe observed.

"Great," said Damont, picking up his ball. "We can finish our game."

"Not with the court all wet," Joe pointed out.

He was concerned that someone might slip and twist an ankle. He had seen that happen to other kids on slippery basketball courts.

"In other words," said Damont, "you're scared you might lose."

"In other words, you're crazy," said Wade, coming to Joe's defense. "Who in their right mind plays on a sloppy, wet court?"

"Anyway," Samantha said diplomatically, "I've got to get home. It's getting pretty close to dinnertime."

"I've got to go home, too," David chimed in.

Fortunately, that was that. Joe thanked Timmy for letting him come over. So did the other kids—all except Damont, of course. Then they left Timmy's house and scattered in different directions and went home.

Joe and David lived on the same block, so they ended up walking together. Wishbone was close behind them.

"So what do you think of Timmy?" David asked his friend.

Joe shrugged. "He seems like a nice guy. Pretty quick, too. Did you see the way he went around Damont?"

David laughed. "Like a bolt of lightning." He paused. "It was nice of him to invite us over."

Joe nodded. By that time, they had come to his house. "I'll see you tomorrow, okay? Come by on the way to school."

"Don't I always?" David asked, grinning. Then he continued on his way.

Joe knelt down and reached out for Wishbone. Taking his cue, the terrier ran into Joe's arms. Joe smiled and scratched Wishbone behind the ears.

"Let's go inside, boy," said Joe. "Mom's making meat loaf tonight. Maybe I can pass you some under the table."

Wishbone loved meat loaf.

When Joe passed him a piece under the table, he enjoyed it the way some people enjoyed a lobster dinner. But as much as he liked meat loaf, he had more of an appetite for the dinnertime conversation than for dinner itself.

"Then what?" asked Joe's mom.

Ellen was an attractive woman with dark hair and smiling eyes. Joe's father had died when Joe was still small. With Wishbone's help, however, Ellen had done a splendid job of raising her son.

"Then," said Joe, "Timmy fell down and scraped his knee. Damont grabbed the ball and dribbled downcourt and tried to score, but I blocked his shot at the last second."

Ellen looked at Joe with concern on her face. "Was Timmy all right?"

Joe nodded. "He was fine. He didn't even get angry at Damont for what he did. In fact, Wade was a lot more angry about it than Timmy was."

His mom nodded. "And you say Timmy's new in town?"

"Yup. He told us he and his parents just moved in the other day."

"Well," said Ellen, "sometimes new kids don't stand up for themselves the way other kids might. They don't want to get anybody angry at them because they don't have any friends yet."

Joe shrugged. "I guess so. Anyway, after that, it started to rain. We went over to Timmy's house and he showed us around his basement. Wow! You should have seen all the old stuff he and his family had down there."

Joe went on to tell his mother about the barber chair and the tin airplanes and the old tennis rackets. Then he described for his mother the trophy Timmy's grandfather had won.

"My," said Ellen, "that *does* sound interesting. I'll bet your dad would have gotten a kick out of seeing that." She wiped her mouth with her napkin and leaned back in her chair. "So, speaking of your dad . . . are you still digging into that box of his mystery novels?"

Just a couple of months ago, Joe and Wishbone had discovered a box of books that had belonged to

Joe's dad. It seemed he had been fascinated by mysteries, because the box was full of them. After Joe had sampled a couple of his dad's favorite whodunits, he had gotten hooked on mysteries, too.

"Actually," Joe told his mother, "I just started a new one. It's called *Peril at End House*, by Agatha Christie."

"Hey," said Wishbone, "that's a good one! One of my favorites, in fact!"

Ellen thought for a moment. "You know, I don't think I ever read that one myself."

Wishbone was surprised. After all, the woman *was* a librarian. He thought she had read every book in print—or close to it.

"I haven't gotten very far into the story yet," Joe noted, "but from what I can tell so far, it's pretty good."

"What's it about?" his mother asked.

"Well," said Joe, "someone in a seaside village called St. Loo is trying to kill a woman named Nick Buckley. She owns an old place called End House. But nobody—including the master detective, Hercule Poirot—has any idea who the killer is, or what he would gain by having Nick dead."

"Sounds interesting," said Ellen.

Joe nodded. "It is. Nick—whose real name is Magdala—doesn't have much money, and her house isn't worth much. So it's hard to figure out why anyone would want to kill her—even the people named in her will. Still, things keep happening to her, but

33

she's able to escape death each time by the skin of her teeth."

"In other words," Wishbone said helpfully, "not by much."

"Then," said Joe, "at Poirot's suggestion, Nick's cousin Maggie comes to stay with her. And when Maggie borrows Nick's red scarf at a fireworks celebration, someone shoots Maggie and kills her."

"Because the killer thought she was Nick?" asked Ellen.

"Exactly," said Joe.

"Hey," said Wishbone, his tail wagging, "tell her more, Joe."

"Then what happens?" asked Ellen.

Joe shrugged. "I don't know, Mom. That's as far as I've gotten."

"Too bad," said Wishbone.

Ellen would simply have to wait to find out the answer to the mystery, just like Joe himself.

The next day was Thursday. As Joe often did, he walked to school with David and Wishbone. Unfortunately, Wishbone couldn't follow them inside.

"Those are the rules," said Joe. "See you later, boy."

Wishbone just sat on the sidewalk leading up to the building and wagged his tail.

Inside the school, Joe and David ran into Samantha. She was bright and cheerful. Then again, Sam was *always* bright and cheerful. In fact, she was the most happy, optimistic person Joe knew. Maybe that was why he liked Sam.

David looked at his watch. "I've got to go, guys. If I hurry, I can put some finishing touches on my science project."

"Okay," said Joe. "See you later."

"Later," Sam echoed.

Out of the corner of his eye, Joe saw someone coming over. He turned and realized it was Timmy. The boy wasn't smiling—far from it, in fact. He looked very worried about something.

"Hi," said Joe.

"What's up?" Sam asked.

Timmy frowned. "I don't know how to say this, but . . . well, you remember the trophies I showed you yesterday?"

"Sure," said Joe.

"Remember the big one?" Timmy continued. "The one with my grandfather's name on it?"

"Of course," said Sam. "What about it?"

Timmy swallowed hard. "It's gone."

Chapter Three

Joe looked at Timmy. "It's *gone?*" he echoed.

"You mean it's not on the shelf?" asked Sam.

"I mean it's not *anywhere*," Timmy said forcefully.

"Hang on," said Joe. "Start at the beginning."

Timmy took a deep breath and then let it out. Doing that calmed him down a bit.

He began again, this time more slowly. "I went downstairs this morning to get some laundry detergent for my mom. On the way, I happened to look in the direction of the trophy shelf—and the big trophy was gone."

"Are you sure it didn't just fall down and roll under some furniture?" Sam asked.

"I'm sure," Timmy told her. "I looked all over for it, but I couldn't find it. It's disappeared."

Joe knew that trophies didn't just vanish into thin air. Nothing did. Someone had to have moved the trophy. "Could your mom have put it somewhere?" he asked.

Timmy shook his head from side to side. "I asked her. She hasn't been down in the basement in a couple of days."

"How about your father?" asked Sam.

"He's out of town," Timmy said.

So someone else had moved the trophy. But who?

Timmy's features hardened. "I hate to say this," he told his new friends, "but I think someone stole that trophy."

"*Stole* it?" Sam repeated. "Are you sure?"

"The window was open," Timmy reminded her. "And when I went outside and looked around, I saw a bunch of sneaker prints in the dirt."

Joe nodded. "The rain made the ground pretty soft," he said.

Soft enough to show that someone had been there. And he couldn't think of a reason for someone to walk around outside Timmy's basement window . . . unless Timmy was right and the trophy *had* been stolen.

"But who would do something like that?" Samantha asked.

Timmy looked at her. "The only people in town who knew about the trophy were the ones I had over yesterday."

Sam thought for a moment, her brow wrinkling

with the effort. "I can't see any of our friends doing that," she said.

"Not even Damont?" Timmy suggested. "He was the one who opened the window, remember? He was also the one who said he would sell the trophies if they were his."

Joe bit his lip. "Damont *has* done some sneaky things," he admitted.

Sam's eyes widened. "Come on, Joe. Damont wouldn't *steal*."

Joe looked at her. "Are you sure about that?"

"He's never stolen anything before," said Sam. "At least," she added in a smaller voice, "not that we know of."

"That's true," Joe replied.

He had known Damont for a long time, and theft was one thing Damont had never been guilty of—at least, until now.

"In any case," Joe said reasonably, "the trophy is gone. That means *someone* took it."

"What am I going to do?" Timmy asked. "My father will kill me if he finds out one of my friends stole that trophy."

"You're exaggerating," Sam said.

"Not by much," Timmy told her.

Joe sympathized with him. "I'll tell you what," he said. "I'll give you a hand. With a little luck, maybe we can find it."

Timmy seemed relieved by the idea. "Thanks," he said.

"Don't mention it," said Joe.

Then the three of them had to end their conversation. It was time for their first class.

Wishbone sat beside Joe's bed, watching his pal lie there and stare at the ceiling, his hands locked behind his head. Ever since Joe had gotten home from school, he had been thinking out loud about Timmy's missing trophy—and Timmy's suspicion that Damont had taken it.

Naturally, Wishbone was interested in helping Joe crack the case. After all, he was a master detective in his own right—when he wasn't digging up the neighbor's yard or chasing squirrels.

"I don't know," Joe said. "I mean, it's certainly possible that Damont took the trophy. On the other hand, I don't have any real proof. And I don't want to accuse him of anything unless I'm sure."

"Good policy," said Wishbone. "Everyone's innocent until proven guilty. Even the Damonster."

Joe thought for a moment. "In *Peril at End House*, the detective Hercule Poirot can't find a convincing suspect among the people present at a murder scene. So what he does is make up an imaginary suspect and call him 'J' for the time being. Then he goes about trying to find evidence to show that 'J' is guilty."

Wishbone tilted his head. "An unusual approach," he admitted. "And yet, I've always found it to be an interesting one."

The terrier found a lot to admire in Hercule Poirot. After all, it was Poirot who said, "The old dog is the one who knows the tricks."

Wishbone wasn't old at all—but then, Poirot wasn't really talking about age. He was talking about experience—something both he and Wishbone had a lot of.

"Until I can gather some evidence," said Joe, "I'm going to do the same thing as Hercule Poirot. I'm going to call my suspect 'J.'" He took a deep breath, then let it out. "And I think I know exactly where I'm going to start my investigation."

Wishbone's tail began to wag. This case was getting exciting.

"Where?" he asked.

"I'm going to check out the footprints that Timmy found outside his basement window." Joe sat up and swung his legs off the bed. "In fact, I'm going to do it right now."

"That's just what I would do," said Wishbone. "Hey, why don't I tag along? When it comes to detective work, footprints are my specialty."

"Come on, boy," said Joe. "We've got work to do."

His tail wagging in a frenzy, Wishbone came right along. "Gee," he said. "I thought you'd never ask."

Joe was glad he'd brought Wishbone along to Timmy's house.

His pal darted around in the bushes the whole way over, flushing squirrels out of hiding and digging up bits of treasure like toy trucks and tennis balls. It made Joe laugh—and at the moment, he needed a good laugh.

Then Joe reached Timmy's house, with its white paint and its black shutters. When he saw Timmy sitting on his front steps with a long, worried face, Joe suddenly didn't feel much like laughing anymore.

"Thanks for coming over," said Timmy.

"No problem," Joe replied. "So where are those footprints?"

"I'll show you," Timmy told him.

He led the way to his backyard. Then he stopped, knelt beside a bare patch of ground, and pointed. Sure enough, there were a couple of sneaker prints visible in the earth.

Joe knelt, too. He touched the prints with his finger. They were dry, but still in good shape. Good enough, in fact, for him to identify the patterns that made up each print.

Joe could see a small oval in the front, surrounded by a ring. There was another oval in the back, where the heel would be, but it didn't have a ring around it. The rest of the print consisted of ridges running diagonally from the area of the big toe to the outside part of the heel.

Wishbone sniffed at the sneaker prints—first one, then the other. But he didn't seem to have any reaction to them.

Joe looked at Timmy. "You're sure no one in your family made these?"

"As sure as I can be," the other boy replied.

Timmy showed Joe the bottom of one of his sneakers. The pattern was different, all right.

"My mom doesn't wear sneakers," Timmy said. "And my dad's foot is a lot bigger than this."

Joe frowned. "So these prints had to have been made by somebody else—a kid, judging by the size of them."

The question was: Who was it? Had Damont left the prints, as Timmy suspected? Or was it someone else?

Joe frowned. He asked himself: *What would Hercule Poirot have done in a situation like this?*

"We need to find out what brand of sneaker has this pattern on its sole," Joe decided. "And I think I know how to do that."

Timmy looked at him. "How?"

"Have you got a piece of paper?" Joe asked him. "And a pencil?"

The other boy shrugged. "I guess so."

"Bring them out," Joe told him. "Then we can copy down the pattern."

"Then what?" asked Timmy.

Joe smiled. "Leave that to me."

Timmy shrugged, then disappeared into his house.

Joe took another look at the prints, then sighed. He hoped they turned out not to belong to anyone he knew. That way, he wouldn't be blowing the whistle on one of his friends.

Wishbone poked his nose into the space between Joe's leg and his arm. The boy laughed and stroked his pal's head.

"Okay, Joe," said Timmy, coming around the corner of his house with a pad full of paper in one hand and a sharpened pencil in the other. "I've got the stuff you asked for."

"Thanks," said Joe.

He opened the pad's cover to the first piece of paper. Then, as carefully as he could, he copied the sneaker pattern with the pencil.

Joe wasn't the best artist in the world—that was for sure. Still, he managed to create a pretty good copy of what he saw in the dirt. He checked it over to make sure he hadn't missed any details. Then he stood up.

"Now what?" asked Timmy.

"Now we visit Oakdale Sports and Games."

Chapter Four

Usually, Joe looked forward to visiting Oakdale Sports & Games. After all, the place was chock-full of everything he loved.

There were racks and bins and stacks of balls everywhere. Baseballs, basketballs, soccer balls, tennis balls—just about every kind of ball a kid could ever want or need.

And that wasn't all. Oakdale Sports & Games stocked bats and helmets and rackets and gloves. It sold shorts and T-shirts and sweatshirts and socks. But most important of all, at least at the moment, it had a large variety of sneakers for sale.

"Wow!" said Timmy, eyes widening as he looked around. "What a great place *this* is."

Wishbone wagged his tail as if to show that he agreed.

Joe walked over to a small glass case in one

corner of the store. Inside it was a newspaper clipping and a pair of track shoes.

"See this?" Joe asked.

Timmy came over and peered into the case. "The article's about a guy named Travis Del Rio."

"That's right," said Joe. "He won the hundred-yard dash in the state track-and-field championships when he was in high school. And these are the shoes he wore when he won it."

Timmy looked a little closer. "He must've been pretty fast, huh?"

"Some people thought so," said a man's voice from in back of them.

Joe turned around and saw a fellow with dark hair and a ready smile. The man also happened to be the owner of Oakdale Sports & Games.

"Travis," said Joe.

Travis clapped the boy on the shoulder. "How's it going, champ?"

Joe shrugged. "Okay, I guess."

Wishbone wagged his tail at the sight of Travis. The store owner laughed and bent down to stroke the terrier's head.

"Good to see you too, boy," said Travis.

Joe jerked a thumb at Timmy. "This is my friend, Timmy Ashbury. He's kind of new in Oakdale."

Travis smiled at Timmy. "Nice to meet you."

"Same here," said Timmy.

"So what brings you to Oakdale Sports and Games?" asked Travis.

Joe frowned. "Well, the truth is . . . I have a problem. Well, actually, it's Timmy's problem. I was hoping you could help us with it."

"Anything you need," said Travis. "I'm your man."

Joe described the trophy to Travis and told him that it had disappeared. Then the boy mentioned the footprints he had seen behind Timmy's house.

"They're our only clue," said Joe.

He pulled a piece of paper out of his pocket. It had the sole pattern he had copied down.

"Can you tell us what kind of sneaker it came from?" asked Joe.

"Yeah," said Timmy, "can you?"

"Well," Travis replied, "I'll be glad to take a look at it."

He accepted Joe's sketch and held it out in front of him. Travis narrowed his eyes. Then he grunted softly.

"Can you identify it?" asked Joe.

"Sure can," said Travis.

"What is it?" asked Timmy.

Travis pointed to the oval in a ring. "See that? It means this shoe is made by Atalan."

Joe had heard of Atalan. It was a popular manufacturer of athletic gear. In fact, just the day before, he had seen a TV commercial for the company's running shoes.

Travis moved his finger down to the oval in the heel area. "This means it's a cross-trainer.

It's a shoe that can be used for a whole bunch of sports."

He ran his fingers along the ridges that extended from toe to heel.

"This diagonal pattern is fairly new. The company has been using it for only the last year or so."

"Can you tell what model it is?" Joe asked hopefully.

Travis handed the sketch back to the boy. "Absolutely."

"You can?" asked Joe.

"Sure," said Travis. "It's a Golden Eagle. It came out a couple of weeks ago. We only received a few pairs of them, and we sold out in a day or two."

"What do they look like?" asked Joe.

"They have a real fancy design," said Travis. "The company really went all out to make this sneaker a bestseller. And it comes in two color combinations—gold-on-black, and gold-on-white."

A chill ran up and down Joe's spine. The sneakers Damont had worn the other day . . . they were gold-on-white, without a doubt.

"Do they have a design of little gold wings on them?" Joe asked.

Travis nodded. "One on the inside and one on the outside."

Joe saw Timmy look at him. Timmy didn't need to say anything, but he said it anyway.

"Those are Damont's sneakers, Joe."

Joe sighed. "It seems that way—at least for now." He turned to Travis. "Thanks for all your help."

Travis flashed a broad smile. "You're welcome. Good luck with solving your mystery, guys."

It was starting to look as if the mystery had already been solved. But Joe didn't say that. What he said to Travis was, "I'll let you know how it all turns out."

Then he led the way out of the store.

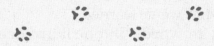

"Uh-oh," said Wishbone, as he followed Joe out of Oakdale Sports & Games. "It looks bad for Damont, all right."

After all, the sneakers Damont was wearing yesterday matched the prints Timmy had found outside his basement window. Joe's "J" suspect now had a name.

In *Peril at End House*, Poirot had been able to give up the "J" approach, as well—when he found out Nick Buckley had become the heir to a great fortune. At that point, Nick's friend Frederica Rice and her cousin Charles Vyse had become prime suspects in the attempts to murder Nick.

Suddenly, Wishbone got a whiff of something interesting. He raised his head and sniffed the air again. The same smell came to him.

"Yup," he said, "no doubt about it."

There was a new dog in the neighborhood.

"What do we do now?" asked Timmy.

Joe thought for a moment. "If Damont took the trophy, he'll probably have it hidden somewhere at his house."

"Good deduction," said Wishbone.

"So we search the place?" Timmy asked.

Joe looked at him. "I don't think Damont's parents would be very happy about that. I'd say our best bet is to go to Damont's house and confront him with what we've learned."

Timmy frowned. "But he'll just deny it."

"Maybe," said Joe. "Then we'll ask him to prove his innocence—by letting us search the places where he might have hidden the trophy."

"What if he doesn't?" asked Timmy.

"Yeah, what if we doesn't?" Wishbone echoed.

Joe sighed. "Then we'll go to his parents. But, first, I'd like to see if we can work this out with Damont."

Wishbone thought that was a good idea. After all, their main objective was to get the trophy back.

"You know," said Joe, "I think we should bring a couple of the other kids in on this."

"What for?" asked Timmy.

"If Damont's taken the trophy and hidden it in his room or something," said Joe, "I want as many witnesses to the fact as possible."

Timmy nodded. "Makes sense."

"Absolutely," Wishbone added.

"I especially want Sam there," said Joe. "You and I and David could be accused of not liking Damont a whole lot, but Sam likes absolutely everyone."

"Okay," said Timmy. "Let's go get them."

The boys started off for Sam's house, which was a bit closer than David's.

"That gives me some time to check out the new guy," said Wishbone.

After all, Joe's case was number one on his list. But if there was going to be a break in the action, he had a strong desire to sniff out case number two.

His decision made, Wishbone put all his attention into following the new dog's scent. It led him up the street and past the gas station. It led him past Henderson Memorial Public Library. Then it led him into one of the residential areas in town.

Of course, it being a breezy day and all, the smell of the new dog seemed to vanish every now and then. But Wishbone was no mere pup—he had been tracking scents for years. Staying on the job and sniffing everything in sight, he eventually picked up the trail again.

Suddenly, Wishbone heard barking. It was still far away, but with his superb sense of hearing it sounded clear as a bell. He stopped for a moment to listen more carefully.

"Two dogs," he said, concentrating. "One I know—my friend Sparky, the golden retriever. He lives in this neck of the woods." He cocked his head to one side. "But the other one . . ."

Instantly, he put two and two together. Unfamiliar scent, unfamiliar voice. They had to belong to the same dog.

And from the tone of the newcomer's voice, it seemed there was trouble between him and Sparky. *Big* trouble.

Sparky was a large dog, but he was gentle to a fault. He wouldn't be able to stand up for himself very well in a fight. That meant he needed a friend to come to his rescue.

Fortunately, Wishbone was just such a friend.

"Here I come!" he told Sparky, launching himself into a flat-out run. "Hang on, old buddy!"

Wishbone ran from yard to yard as fast as his four powerful legs would carry him. He ducked under fences and leaped over others. He ran around bushes when he could, and squirmed through them when he couldn't. At long last, he made his way into Sparky's yard.

That was when he saw the Brute.

He was a big, dark, muscular dog, with a flat head, a huge chest, and scary, light-colored eyes. Worse, he had one of Sparky's rawhide chew toys in his mouth—the one that looked like a bone with a bow around it.

Sparky was barking at the Brute at the top of his lungs. Every so often he would jump forward as if he was going to try to recover his chew toy.

But when the newcomer eyed him with those pale, spooky eyes of his, Sparky jumped right back again.

It was a good thing, too. Sparky was no match for the stranger.

"All right," said Wishbone, making his presence felt. "Let's see you pick on someone your own size—more or less."

The Brute turned and looked at him. For just a moment, Wishbone thought the big dog was going to drop the chew toy and jump on him, instead.

Then the terrier heard a shrill, high-pitched sound. He had heard that type of sound before. It had come from a dog whistle.

Obviously, Sparky and the Brute had heard the whistle, too. They were looking in the direction from which it had come.

Suddenly, the big dog dropped the chew toy—though by that time, he had mangled it pretty badly—and trotted off. Apparently, the whistle was meant for *him*.

What luck, Wishbone thought. If that whistle had come a little later, he might have had his paws full with the newcomer.

But before the big dog left the yard, he turned and gave Wishbone a dirty look—as if to say, "Don't think you've seen the last of me, because you haven't."

Finally, with a snuffle, the Brute left Sparky's yard.

Wishbone rushed to Sparky's side. "Are you okay?" he asked his friend.

The golden retriever turned to look at Wishbone with his big brown eyes. He wagged his tail.

"I'll take that as a 'yes,'" Wishbone said.

Sparky padded over to his chew toy, which the Brute had torn up and slobbered over, and sniffed it sadly for a few moments. Then he turned his back on it, as if it were no longer anything for which he had any affection.

"I'd feel the same way if it were mine," Wishbone said in sympathy.

Sparky wagged his tail in response.

"I agree," said Wishbone. "It isn't fair. That toy belonged to you, Sparky. The Brute had no right to mangle it that way."

Wishbone wished he had gotten there before

the Brute had dug his big, old paws into the toy. Of course, it might not have made a difference— and then again, maybe it would have.

In any case, one thing was certain—the big dog would be back.

Chapter Five

As Joe walked down the street to Damont's house, with Timmy on one side of him and Sam and David on the other, he was confident he had made the right decision by asking Sam and David to come along.

After all, this was a pretty serious mission they were on. Joe wanted to make sure he was doing it right.

Finally, the four of them reached Damont's house. For a moment, they just stood there on the sidewalk, looking at it.

Sam sighed. "This is silly," she said.

"But necessary," David reminded her.

She frowned. "I guess."

Sam had agreed to go along because she wanted to clear Damont's name of any wrong- doing. If he was as innocent as she thought he was, they would know that soon enough.

But if he was guilty, they would know that, too.

Joe took a deep breath. Then he led the way up the walk to Damont's house. His three friends followed. Suddenly, with a blur of speed, a fourth friend joined him.

It was Wishbone!

Joe knelt and scratched Wishbone behind the ears. "Hey, boy," he said. "Where have you been?"

Wishbone didn't say. He just licked Joe's face, his tail wagging wildly. It was as if Wishbone was eager to get on with the investigation.

Joe was glad Wishbone had shown up. He felt better when his pal was at his side.

Standing up, Joe walked the rest of the way to Damont's front door and rang the bell. However, he didn't get any response. After a few seconds, he rang the bell again.

This time, someone answered. As luck would have it, it was Damont himself. He looked at the kids with a hint of surprise in his crooked smile.

"What's going on?" Damont asked. "You getting together a basketball game, or is the candy sale starting early this year?"

"We're not getting together a game," Joe replied.

"And this is a bit more serious than the candy sale," David noted in a humorless voice.

"Maybe to *you*," said Damont. "I really like candy. Especially the chocolatey kind. In fact—"

"Damont!" Sam interrupted. "This isn't a laughing matter."

Damont always listened to Sam better than he listened to anyone else. "Okay," he said, "no problem. What's on your mind?"

Joe frowned. "One of Timmy's trophies is missing."

Damont seemed surprised. "Oh, yeah?"

"The really nice one," Timmy added. "The one you thought would be worth a lot of money."

"That's too bad," said Damont. "But why are you telling *me?*"

That was when Joe mentioned the basement window Damont opened, and the sneaker prints Timmy found in the backyard. Then he told Damont he had taken a sketch of the prints to Oakdale Sports & Games.

"So what?" asked Damont.

"So Travis described the sneakers that made those prints," said David. He pointed to Damont's sneakers. "And you're wearing them."

Damont looked down at his white-and-gold cross-trainers. When he looked up at David again, he had a funny expression on his face. "What are you saying? That *I* took the trophy?"

"Are you going to deny it?" David asked.

Damont laughed. "You *bet* I'm going to deny it!"

"What about your sneaker prints?" asked Timmy.

"I don't care *what* Travis told you," Damont insisted. "I wasn't anywhere near the backyard of your house. And I definitely did not steal any trophy."

"Prove it," said David.

Damont looked at him narrow-eyed. "Prove it *how?*"

"By letting us search the premises."

"The premises?" Damont repeated. "You mean my whole house?"

"For starters, maybe just your room," Joe suggested.

Damont frowned. "Let me get this straight. You want to search my room—my *bedroom*—for Timmy's grandfather's trophy?"

"That's right," said David.

Damont thought for a moment. Then he shrugged. "Sure, why not? I've got nothing to hide."

With that, he led the way into the house and up the stairs to his room. When they got there, he turned around and held his arms out.

"Okay," said Damont, "where do we start?"

For a moment, Joe was surprised. Then, he shrugged and followed Damont inside.

Damont's room was neat and carefully furnished. Like Damont himself, it seemed to put on a false face. There were only a few things in the whole room that reflected Damont's personality. One of those things was an in-your-face poster of Damont's favorite basketball star.

"Well?" said Damont.

"How about the dresser drawers?" asked Joe.

"Fine with me," said Damont.

61

He opened them all, one at a time. There was no trophy in any of them. In fact, there was nothing in them even resembling a trophy.

"What's next?" asked Damont. "Under the bed?"

David got down on his hands and knees and looked. He came up shaking his head.

"Not there, either," he said.

"Hey, how about the closet?" asked Damont. "That would be a great place to stow a trophy!"

Joe frowned. "Maybe it would be."

Damont opened his closet door and revealed a closet stuffed with junk. Not bothered by the mess, the kids started sorting through it. Wishbone helped, too, sniffing everything he could find.

Damont watched them the whole time, his arms crossed over his chest. He looked more and more triumphant with each passing moment.

"What's the matter?" he said at last. "Having trouble, guys? Maybe I can give you a hand."

"It's not here," Timmy concluded.

"Then it's somewhere else," said David. "Let's try the garage." He looked at Damont. "Unless you don't want us looking there."

"Go right ahead," Damont told him. By then, he had a big smile on his face. "To tell you the truth, this is more fun than playing a video game."

Leading the way again, he went back down the stairs and through the kitchen. Then he opened the door that led to his family's garage and flipped a switch to turn on the lights.

"Hey," said Damont, "while you're in here, maybe you can straighten things up a little. The place is a real mess."

Joe took a look and saw that Damont wasn't kidding. The Jones family didn't keep their car in their garage, but they seemed to keep just about everything else there.

Joe saw an old refrigerator, a couple of little kids' bicycles, a rowing machine with a handle missing, several cans of paint, a card table, a broken-down sewing machine, a gas barbecue, three or four rakes, and a stack of water-damaged magazines.

And that was just the tip of the iceberg.

There were birdhouses, a bunch of cardboard boxes, a lawn sprinkler, some hardcover books, a snow shovel, a gardening glove, some videotapes, a deflated football, a picture frame missing its glass, some plastic bottles, and a big pile of toy trucks.

"You sure you want to do this?" Damont asked.

David rolled up his sleeves. "Come on, gang," he said with determination. "Let's dig in."

And that was exactly what they did. Little by little, they sifted through the mountains of junk. Wishbone slipped into places the rest of them couldn't easily get through, but he didn't come up with anything.

Damont just stood in a corner and looked smug.

After about twenty minutes, Joe was starting to think this search hadn't been such a good idea. After all, if Damont had stolen the trophy and hidden it there in his garage, why would he be so calm and cooperative about letting them rummage through the place?

In part of Joe's mind, he felt relief. After all, he really didn't want to believe Damont was a thief.

Then something happened.

Half hidden from Joe by a stack of cardboard boxes, Sam made a sound of surprise. Then she stood up, a funny look on her face.

"What is it?" asked David.

Sam bent down again, then straightened and held something up. It was long and slender, and it glinted in the light.

"My grandfather's trophy!" Timmy exclaimed.

Rushing over to Sam, he took it from her. Then he showed it to the rest of them, so there would be no mistake.

"This is it!" he said.

Joe turned to Damont. The boy's mouth had dropped open. Damont looked around, his eyes widening.

"You don't think . . ." he said.

"Oh, yes, we *do*," David replied.

"Wait a minute," Damont said, holding his hands up in front of his chest. "I don't have any idea of how that thing got here. I'm telling you the truth!"

"Oh, sure," David responded. "Just like you always do."

"But I am!" Damont insisted. "I didn't steal that trophy, guys. I haven't even seen it since we left Timmy's basement!"

This time, even Sam was hard-pressed to defend him. She didn't say anything. She just looked sad.

"Come on," said David. "Let's get out of here."

He left the garage first. Then came Timmy, his trophy held securely in his hands. Sam followed with a disappointed look on her face.

"Guys," Damont groaned, "I didn't do it." He looked at Joe. "You've *got* to believe me—it wasn't me."

Joe studied Damont's face. The boy had never seemed more sincere. But then, it was difficult to tell with Damont.

Finally, Joe turned to Wishbone and said, "Come on, boy." Together, they followed the others out of the garage.

"Hoo, boy," said Wishbone, as he and his pal Joe caught up with the other kids at the bottom of Damont's driveway. "The Damonster looks pretty guilty, all right."

Of course, appearances could be deceiving. As a master detective, the Jack Russell terrier knew that only too well.

"Well," said David, "I guess that's that. I had a feeling Damont was guilty all along."

Being a guy who liked to work with machines, David was always more comfortable when the pieces fit. This time was no exception, Wishbone thought.

Sam was different, though. "I don't know," she said. "Maybe I'm out of my mind, but . . ."

"But what?" said Joe.

His friend shrugged. "I still believe Damont when he says he didn't steal the trophy."

"You do?" said David disbelievingly.

Sam nodded. "I know we found the trophy in Damont's garage and everything, but that doesn't mean he took it for sure. It's just . . . what do they call it? Circumstantial evidence—there's no definite proof."

Joe frowned.

Sam eyed him. "You don't believe it either, do you?"

Joe sighed. "I wish I could," he said. "But . . ."

"But what?" asked Sam.

Joe shook his head. "Damont taking that trophy . . . it doesn't sound right to me somehow. I can't describe it, but it doesn't *fit.*"

"Hang on a second!" came a voice from behind them.

Wishbone turned and saw Damont running after them along the sidewalk. The Damonster came around Joe, David, Timmy, and Samantha and stopped directly in front of them.

"What is it now?" David asked.

"I didn't do it," Damont insisted. "But I think I know who *did.*"

Joe looked at him. "Who?"

"Wade," said Damont.

"Wade?" Sam echoed.

"That's right. I saw him hanging out in front of my house this morning. He could have stolen the trophy and put it in the garage."

"But why would Wade want to do that?"

asked Timmy. "Why would he steal the trophy and then put it in your garage?"

Damont held his hands out, palms upward. "Give me a break, will you? To frame me, of course."

David folded his arms across his chest. "Oh, sure," he said.

Damont looked at Joe and Samantha. "Don't you ever watch any of the detective shows on TV? People are always framing other people for crimes they didn't commit."

"What happens on TV and what happens in real life are two different things," David pointed out.

"But Wade's got it in for me," Damont replied. "You heard what he said on the basketball court, didn't you?"

Wishbone remembered. But then, he remembered everything.

Joe stroked his chin. "Now that I think of it, Wade *did* say something on the court."

"He did?" asked David.

Joe nodded. "Something about Damont always getting his way."

"Good memory, Joe," said Wishbone.

"That's right," said Damont. "And then he said he was going to get even with me."

"Actually," Sam told him, "Wade said *someone* was going to get even with you. He didn't say it was going to be *him*."

"Hey," said Damont, "that's close enough, isn't it?"

"What about the sneaker prints?" asked David.

"He saw me wearing my Atalans," Damont said. "He could have found a pair and made all those prints with them."

"Not likely," said David.

"But *possible,*" Damont pointed out. He turned to Joe. "Am I right?"

Wishbone looked up at Joe, too. The boy seemed to be giving Damont's argument some consideration.

"I'd do the same thing, Joe," said Wishbone. "Listen to your inner detective—that's what Hercule Poirot always did. If he had a hunch, he went with it."

Joe frowned. "All right," he said at last. "I'll check out Wade's story."

Damont grinned his lopsided grin. "You won't regret it, Joe. You'll see that it was Wade who took that trophy."

Wishbone snorted. "Maybe," he said. "Only time and good detective work will tell."

Chapter Six

The next morning, which was Friday, Wishbone kept Joe and David company as they walked to school. Every step of the way, they talked about how Joe was going to approach Wade with Damont's accusation.

"Just come right out and tell him about it," said Wishbone.

Poirot always did that. He learned a lot from people's immediate reactions.

"Maybe you could peek inside Wade's locker first," David suggested. "He never locks it, you know. You could see if he has any of those special sneakers in there."

Joe made a face. "I couldn't just look into his locker."

"Just *tell* him," Wishbone repeated.

"You know," said Joe, "I think I'm just going to tell him what Damont said—and then see how he reacts."

"There you go," said the terrier, his tail wagging furiously. "Who says great minds don't think alike?"

A moment later, they arrived at Joe and David's school. Unfortunately, as Wishbone had been told often enough, dogs weren't allowed inside the building—not even the kind that had one brown ear and one speckled ear and knew Shakespeare's works inside and out.

Normally, that rule bothered Wishbone a bit. But not today. Today, he had some business of his own to attend to.

"See ya later, boy," said Joe, bending down to stroke his pal's fur. Then he and David disappeared inside the school building.

"Later," Wishbone echoed.

Then he turned and started off in the direction of Sparky's backyard. After all, the golden retriever had seemed pretty down the day before. And if there was anything Wishbone was good at, it was cheering people up—especially if those people were dogs.

It didn't take long to get to Sparky's place. But when Wishbone arrived, he saw his friend sporting a long face. It was only when the retriever saw Wishbone that his tail began to wag.

"What's the matter?" Wishbone asked.

Even before he had finished the question, he had an idea what the answer might be. But just in case the terrier had any doubts, he saw the evidence in the cool, shadowy closeness of Sparky's doghouse.

There was Sparky's pile of rawhide chew toys—by far the biggest collection in the neighborhood. Wishbone scanned the pile with a critical eye.

He saw half a dozen toys, from make-believe bones to baseballs to flying saucers. But one toy was missing. It was Sparky's favorite, too—a piece of rawhide twisted into the shape of a pretzel.

Wishbone snorted. "And I know who took it."

Obviously, it was the Brute. His scent was still floating around in Sparky's doghouse, telling Wishbone that the big dog had been there not more than a couple of hours ago.

"Boy," said Wishbone. "This dog doesn't waste any time making good on his threats."

The day before, the Brute had mangled one of Sparky's toys. Now he had stolen the pretzel as well—no doubt, so he could grind it down to nothing at his leisure.

Wishbone looked at Sparky. The golden retriever wagged his tail with frustration. Obviously, he missed his chew toy. But, more important, he felt humiliated that the Brute had gotten the best of him again.

Sparky didn't actually come out and say that, of course. But then, he didn't have to.

"Something's got to be done," Wishbone said.

Sparky wagged his tail again. Apparently, he felt the same way.

Unfortunately, the retriever wasn't allowed to leave his owners' backyard. He couldn't track the Brute to find out the fate of his chew toy.

But Wishbone wasn't held back by that kind of restriction. He could follow the big dog to his home—wherever that was—then find the pretzel-shaped chew toy and get it back.

And that was just what he would do. After all, Oakdale was *his* town, *his* special place. He couldn't just stand around and let the Brute threaten the local canine residents.

Wishbone barked and got Sparky to look up at him. "Crime doesn't pay," he told the golden retriever. "At least, if I have anything to say about it—and fortunately for you, old buddy, I do."

Walking down the school hallway, Joe thought about his four-legged pal. Wishbone had scurried off as if he had important business to attend to.

Of course, Joe had to attend to some pretty important business of his own. He wasn't looking forward to it much, either.

When he promised Timmy he would help him find his grandfather's trophy, he had imagined his job would end with the trophy's recovery. He didn't think he would still be investigating the matter after the trophy was safely back where it belonged.

But that was just what he was doing. And it was all because he didn't believe Damont was guilty, no matter how clearly the evidence was stacked up against him.

It wasn't logical. But then, a detective had to follow his instincts sometimes.

"Hey, Joe," said David. "There's Wade."

Joe followed his friend's pointing finger. Sure enough, Wade was halfway down the hall, talking with a couple of other guys. As Joe watched, the others moved away, leaving Wade all by himself for a moment.

That was Joe's chance. He took it.

Weaving his way down the hall past groups of other kids, he waved to Wade. With luck, Joe thought, the blond boy would see him and stay where he was. A moment later, Wade noticed him and waved back.

"How's it going?" he asked as Joe and David approached him.

"Not bad," said Joe.

"Pretty good, actually," David added.

Joe frowned. "Listen, Wade, there's something I've got to ask you."

"Sure," said Wade. "Go ahead."

Joe looked the other boy in the eye. "You remember Timmy's grandfather's trophy? The really cool one? Well, it was stolen out of Timmy's basement after we left the other day."

"Stolen?" Wade echoed. "Are you sure?"

Joe nodded. "Fortunately, we found the trophy yesterday. It was in Damont's garage."

Wade's eyes narrowed. "Then Damont was the one who took it?"

Joe shrugged his shoulders. "It looks that way. Of course, he says it wasn't him."

Wade grunted. "He *would* say that."

"Actually," said Joe, "he told me someone was hanging around his house the other day—someone who might have stolen the trophy and then put it in Damont's garage when no one was looking."

"What for?" asked Wade.

"To get him in trouble," David explained.

Wade's brow creased. "Sounds fishy. I mean, I was on Damont's block yesterday, and I didn't see—"

He stopped in mid-sentence. Then his expression changed from curiosity to anger.

"Wait a second! Are you accusing *me* of stealing that trophy? And then trying to make it look like Damont did it?"

Joe shook his head from side to side. "I'm not accusing you of anything. But I promised Damont I would ask you about it."

Wade's mouth became a hard, straight line. "Then you *are* accusing me of stealing the trophy."

"*Damont* accused you," said David.

"Then Damont should have done it to my face," Wade replied.

Before Joe could say anything more, Wade stalked off down the hall. Joe watched him go.

"What do you think?" asked David.

Joe turned to his friend. "I'm not sure."

"He sure *acted* as if he was innocent," said David.

Joe nodded. "That's true. But he didn't say what he was doing on Damont's block yesterday."

David's eyes opened wide. "That's right, he didn't. And he could have cleared himself right then and there if he'd told us that."

"Then again," Joe thought out loud, "Wade might not have thought he owed us an explanation. I mean, we're not the police or anything."

"So now what?" asked David.

It was a good question.

As far as Joe was concerned, the evidence still pointed to Damont. But after this morning, Joe had to consider Wade a suspect, too.

At least he didn't have to stick with Hercule Poirot's strategy of pursuing a mysterious "J." Joe no longer had a shortage of possible culprits.

His only question now was: Which of them had stolen the trophy?

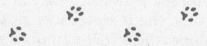

Wishbone didn't have any doubts as to who stole his friend Sparky's chew toy. His only question was: Where was the Brute hiding it?

To Wishbone's sharp-thinking mind, there was only one way to answer that question. Anyway, that was what he told Sparky when he went to visit his friend later in the day.

"You see," said Wishbone, "a criminal always returns to the scene of the crime. Every self-respecting detective knows that. So all I have to do is hide out here in your backyard until the big dog shows up, then follow him back to his home."

Sparky wagged his tail—no doubt, a sign that he was interested in Wishbone's plan.

"And his home," Wishbone added, "is where I'll find your pretzel toy. I'd stake my career on it."

Sparky wagged his tail again. Obviously, he liked that idea, too.

"All right," said Wishbone. "I'm going to hide in the bushes upwind of your doghouse, so the Brute doesn't sniff me out when he shows up."

Sparky wagged his tail yet again, as if to say, "What do *I* do?"

"I'm glad you asked," said the terrier. "You do exactly what you did before—bark a lot and look angry. That way, the big dog won't suspect he's walking into a stakeout. Got it?"

As before, Sparky wagged his tail.

Apparently, the retriever was all set. Leaving his friend alone, the terrier withdrew to a spot in the bushes upwind of Sparky's house.

Then he shifted around in the soft soil until he got himself good and comfortable. "There," he said. "That ought to do it. Now it's just a matter of waiting until the Brute takes the bait."

Having done this sort of thing before, Wishbone knew that it might take a while. He was prepared for that—or so he thought. But several hours went by, and there was still no sign of the big dog.

"This is starting to get a little boring," he said. "In the time I've been sitting here, I could have dug up Wanda's garden two or three times and chased half a dozen squirrels."

Still, Wishbone didn't move. He stayed right where he was, eyes and ears alert, nose sniffing the air for the big dog's scent.

A good detective must be patient, he thought. He must never give up, no matter how winding and disappointing a trail he must follow.

At least, that was what Hercule Poirot said in *Peril at End House,* as he was trying to track down Maggie Buckley's killer.

Wishbone recalled the master detective's exact words: "Hercule Poirot is a good dog. The dog follows the scent, and if, regrettably, there is no scent to follow, he noses around—seeking always something that is not very nice. So, also, does Hercule Poirot. And often—oh! so often—does he find it!"

Suddenly, Wishbone's patience paid off. He caught a whiff of the scent he was looking for. Then another whiff. And a few seconds later, he saw the Brute that went with it.

It was the same bruiser he had seen before— spooky, pale eyes and all. Wishbone hunkered down

in his hiding place, trying his best not to draw the big fellow's attention.

His strategy seemed to work, too. The big dog didn't even glance in his direction as he entered the yard. He just trotted over to Sparky's doghouse as if he owned it and everything in it.

Sparky barked at the Brute's appearance, but he didn't make a move to stop the intruder when he poked his head into the doghouse.

"Right according to plan," Wishbone said.

For a moment, the Brute buried his large bulk in the shadowy depths of the place. When he came out again, he had something in his big, toothy mouth. It was another of Sparky's chew toys, of course—the one that looked like a football.

Sparky barked even louder, but it didn't bother the Brute one little bit. He glanced casually at the golden retriever, then padded back in the direction he had come from, the football clamped firmly in his jaw.

So far, so good, thought Wishbone.

Unaware that he was being watched by anyone except Sparky, the big dog slipped out of the backyard. Wishbone waited until the Brute was completely out of sight. Then he crept out from his hiding place.

Sparky wagged his tail at the sight of his friend. It had to be humiliating for the golden retriever to watch the big dog come into his yard and take whatever he wanted, trap or no trap.

"I feel your pain," Wishbone said.

Then, careful to stay upwind so the big dog didn't catch his scent, the terrier detective went off after the thief. With a little luck, he thought, Sparky wouldn't be looking sad for much longer.

Chapter Seven

The Brute led Wishbone on a wild chase through Oakdale. They wound their way through the streets and backyards of Sparky's neighborhood, then made their way toward the center of town.

All along the way, Wishbone was careful to stay upwind of his quarry. Whenever the Brute started to look back over his shoulder, Wishbone ducked behind a hedge or a nice, thick oak tree.

In fact, it was like a big game of hide-and-seek—except, in this case, Wishbone was doing the hiding as well as the seeking. That made the whole job a little more difficult.

Before long, the Brute scampered past the library. Then he continued past the gas station, Snook's Furniture, and Oakdale Sports & Games.

"Lead on," said Wishbone, eagerly accepting the challenge.

Fortunately, he knew downtown Oakdale like

the back of his paw. When it came to staying out of sight, he was able to take advantage of every corner and streetlamp, every bush and every doorway.

He was just padding past the office of the *Oakdale Chronicle,* the town newspaper, when he heard someone cry out, "Yoo-hoo! Wishbone!"

The terrier looked around nervously. Who was calling him? The last thing he wanted was to draw attention to himself and make the Brute suspect he was being followed.

"Yoo-hoo!" someone cried again.

I know that voice, Wishbone told himself.

Suddenly, he caught sight of its owner. It was Wanda Gilmore, Joe and Ellen's next-door neighbor. She was coming out of Rosie's Rendezvous Books & Gifts, the little shop across the street.

"Wishbone!" she called out.

Wanda wasn't always so happy to see him. After all, Wishbone had dug up her flower garden a few times. Well, maybe *more* than a few times. But at the moment, the woman seemed to have forgotten all that.

"Sorry," he told Wanda. "Don't want to be rude, but I've got to run. See you in the petunia bed." Then he ran past Rosie's and Dart Animal Clinic before the Brute could get too big a lead on him.

"Wishbone!" Wanda cried. "Oh, Wishbone!"

But he kept going, zigging and zagging from one side of the street to the other. To his relief, the

Brute didn't seem to notice Wanda's calls. He just kept going, eyes straight ahead.

But where was the big dog leading him? That was what Wishbone really wanted to know.

The Brute didn't stop at Beck's Grocery. He didn't stop at Pepper Pete's, the pizza place owned by Samantha's father. But once he passed Pepper Pete's, he made a left turn.

A few moments later, Wishbone made a left turn, too. By then, the Brute was already in line with the First Commerce Bank of Oakdale. And as far as Wishbone could tell, the big dog was still nowhere near his destination.

The Brute continued a little farther—then paused in front of the Oakdale Attic Antiques shop. Wishbone hid behind one of the stone pillars in front of the bank, waiting for his quarry to start forward again.

But the big dog didn't do anything of the sort. He just stood there, looking around for a moment. Suddenly, the door to the antiques store was opened by someone and the Brute went inside.

"Ah-ha!" said Wishbone.

He knew he had to follow the Brute into the store at all costs. Otherwise, he might never find out where the big bully had hidden Sparky's chew toys.

With that in mind, Wishbone darted for Oakdale Attic Antiques, his four legs churning as fast as they could. The shop's door was beginning to swing closed, but its spring assembly was keeping it from closing too quickly. If the terrier didn't slow down even for a second, he had a chance to make it inside.

"Come on," he said, "you can do it—I mean, *I* can do it!"

It was going to be close. Digging deep down into his reserve of energy, Wishbone applied an extra burst of speed—and managed to dart inside just before the door slammed shut.

That was the good news. The bad news was that he ran into something, too—and what he ran into was a man's leg.

Looking up, Wishbone recognized the man as Mr. Hubbard, the owner of the antiques store. Mr. Hubbard was a heavyset fellow with wavy, gray hair and thick glasses. He looked down at Wishbone in surprise.

"Oh, no, you don't," he said. "Come on, boy. We don't allow dogs in here."

"Er . . . you don't?" said Wishbone. He tried to catch a glimpse of the Brute in the store, but was unsuccessful. "Then how come you let in that musclebound thief with my friend's chew toy in his mouth?"

It was a fair question. Unfortunately, it didn't seem that Wishbone was going to get a satisfactory answer. In fact, it didn't seem he was going to get any answer at all.

"Come on," said Mr. Hubbard. "Shoo!"

"But I'm in the middle of an important investigation!" Wishbone protested. "This is official detective business!"

The store owner opened the door, then bent down and pushed the master detective outside. Then he shut the door behind Wishbone, took hold of a sign hanging from a suction cup on the back of the door—and flipped it over.

Wishbone knew what that sign meant: the store was closed for the day. It wouldn't open again until the following morning.

Of course, he didn't want to *wait* until the following morning. He wanted to go after the Brute and close the case right then and there.

Placing his paws on the glass of the door, Wishbone stood up on his hind legs and barked—for all the good it did. Locking the door from the inside, the shopkeeper turned and walked away.

"Don't look so pleased with yourself," Wishbone told Mr. Hubbard. "I've been thrown out of better places, you know."

Unfortunately, that didn't help Sparky. His football toy was gone, just like his pretzel toy. And there was nothing Wishbone or anyone else could do about it.

"Wait a minute," said Wishbone. "What am I talking about?"

Tomorrow was another day. And now that he knew where the big dog could be found, he was a step closer to his objective.

"I've got to remember Hercule Poirot's advice and be patient," he reminded himself. "After all, Rome wasn't built in a day."

A plan began to take shape in his razor-sharp detective's mind. Well, maybe just the *beginning* of a plan.

Mr. Hubbard had said he didn't allow pets in his antiques store—probably to keep things from being broken. But if Wishbone could get Joe to come to the store, that might be a different story. Then the terrier could snoop around and maybe find Sparky's stuff.

The only problem was how to get Joe down here. "Hmm," said Wishbone, looking around. "If only there were some kind of—"

And then he spotted the very thing he needed, lying there on the sidewalk outside the antiques store.

"Yes!" Wishbone exclaimed, flipping head over paws in celebration of his unexpectedly good fortune.

He picked the thing up in his mouth. Then he headed for home, hoping that what he had found would be enough to get Joe to help him.

Joe knelt outside Timmy's basement window and inspected the sneaker prints he had seen in the ground the other day. It hadn't rained in a while, so the prints were still pretty easy to identify.

The boy pulled out the piece of paper from his back pocket and unfolded it—to reveal the sketch he had made. That was still sharp as well. As carefully as he could, he compared the sketch to the sneaker prints.

"Well?" asked Timmy, who was hunkered down beside him.

Joe shook his head. "They still match," he concluded.

Timmy looked at him. "I don't understand why you're trying to help Damont. He's guilty, Joe. We found the trophy in his garage."

"I know we did," said Joe. "But I just can't get myself to believe he took the trophy. Something about it doesn't add up. Besides, Wade confirmed he was on Damont's block before we found the trophy. So maybe there's something to Damont's suspicions about Wade after all."

"You really think Wade tried to frame Damont?" asked Timmy.

Joe looked at him. "To tell you the truth, I don't know what to believe. I just wish I could find out this was all some kind of mix-up. I don't like thinking either of those guys is a thief."

Timmy nodded. "I can imagine. I mean, I just met them the other day, but it's hard for me, too."

Joe got up and brushed off his knees. "I guess I ought to go home now," he said. "It's almost dinnertime."

"Okay," Timmy replied. "I'll see you tomorrow."

"Yeah," said Joe. "See you."

He had almost rounded the corner of Timmy's house when he heard Timmy call his name. He turned around.

"What is it?" Joe asked.

Timmy smiled gratefully. "Thanks again—for finding my grandfather's trophy, I mean."

Joe smiled back. "No problem," he said. Then he headed for home.

On the way, he thought some more about the mystery of who had taken the trophy. *Maybe Timmy's right,* he thought. *Maybe Damont is guilty after all, and confronting Wade was a waste of time.*

Unfortunately, Joe couldn't get himself to feel the case was closed. The evidence against Damont was pretty strong, but as Sam had pointed out, it was really just circumstantial.

In other words, it didn't prove anything for

certain. It just made it seem more likely that Damont was the guilty party.

In *Peril at End House,* the evidence against Nick Buckley's friend, Frederica Rice, had been circumstantial as well. Nick had received a box of chocolates from her, and the chocolates had turned out to be poisoned.

But Poirot hadn't believed Mrs. Rice was guilty. His instincts told him that someone else had poisoned the chocolates before they got to Nick Buckley.

Joe sighed. He would feel a lot better if he could just get one more bit of proof. Then he could apologize to Wade and wash his hands of the whole incident.

Suddenly, Joe heard barking. It wasn't just any barking, either. It was a barking he had come to know quite well.

A moment later, he saw Wishbone round a corner and come bounding toward him. Joe knelt and scratched the back of Wishbone's neck.

"Hi, boy," he said. "Am I glad to see you!"

Wishbone stuck his nose in Joe's face. It was only then that the boy noticed his pal was clutching something in his mouth.

It was a business card of some kind. Joe took it out of Wishbone's mouth and looked at it more closely.

The card was a little soggy and chewed up,

but Joe could still read it. It had the name, address, phone number, and hours of Oakdale Attic Antiques. In fact, Joe realized, it was the same kind of card Timmy had shown the kids in his basement the other day.

He looked at Wishbone. "Where did you get this, boy?"

Wishbone couldn't answer, of course.

At first, Joe thought Wishbone had just found it on the street somewhere.

But as Joe gazed at the card, something clicked in his brain. "Wait a minute," he said. "Oakdale Attic . . ."

Wishbone's tail wagged. Joe stroked his pal's head.

"You know what?" said Joe. "You've just

given me an idea—one that might help me solve this mystery."

Of course, it could lead him to the conclusion that Damont was guilty after all. But like Poirot, Joe just wanted to get to the truth of the matter.

Chapter Eight

Wishbone couldn't wait any longer.

With a quick bound, he landed on Joe's bed and licked his face. The boy put a hand up to stop his pal, but the terrier kept licking, refusing to give up. Finally, Joe sat up in bed.

"What is it?" he asked Wishbone, blinking at the early morning light streaming in through his bedroom window.

"What is it?" Wishbone echoed. "I'll tell you what it is. It's Saturday—and the antiques store opens in half an hour."

Joe flipped his blanket aside and swung his legs out of bed. Then he opened his mouth and yawned.

"Man, oh, man," he said. "I couldn't sleep all night, Wishbone. I was thinking about getting down to Oakdale Attic Antiques to see if Mr. Hubbard can help me with the mystery."

He reached over to his bedside table and picked up the wrinkled business card that Wishbone had brought him the day before. Then he studied it, as if the card alone would tell him just what he needed to know.

"Of course," Joe said, in a slow, thoughtful voice, "I might not learn anything at all at the antiques store. But it's still a lead, and I've got to check it out."

"Absolutely right," said Wishbone. "*We've* got to check it out. And while we're doing that, I'll see if I can find out where the Brute's hidden Sparky's chew toys."

Things had worked out a lot better than Wishbone had planned. He had hoped just to plant the thought of visiting the store in Joe's mind. It was sheer luck that the boy had seen an advantage in going there as well.

Joe fell back on his bed and stretched out his arms. He yawned once again. Joe was about as tired as Wishbone had ever seen him. The terrier jumped on top of the boy and started licking his face even harder than before.

"Rise and shine, Joe!" he said.

Then he leaped off the bed and landed with all four feet on the wooden floor, his tail wagging back and forth with real excitement. He couldn't wait to get into that antiques store and snoop around.

After all, how often did he get the chance to solve *two* crimes at once?

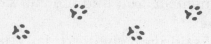

Joe got down to the kitchen before his mother did, made himself a breakfast of cereal with milk, and downed it in record time. He was just starting to clear away his dishes when his mom entered the kitchen.

Ellen looked at Joe as if he had grown a knee-length polka-dot beard. "Who are you?" she asked. "And what have you done with my son? He *never* gets up this early."

Joe shrugged. "I wanted to get over to the antiques store, Mom. It opens early on Saturdays." He glanced at Wishbone. "Besides," he added, "a certain character wouldn't let me stay in bed."

His mother looked at him in a questioning way. "Oakdale Attic Antiques?"

Joe nodded. "Uh-huh."

"What's so interesting there?" Ellen asked.

Joe shot her an apologetic look. "It's kind of a long story, Mom."

"I've got some time," she told him.

Joe could tell that he wasn't going to get out of the house without giving his mother an explanation. He plunked himself down in his chair.

"You see," he said, "it all started the other day, when our game got rained out and we went over to Timmy's house."

His mom sat down at the opposite side of the

95

table. "I remember. You told me you saw all those neat antiques."

"Well," said Joe, "the next day, Timmy came over to me in school and told me one of the antiques had disappeared—the basketball trophy that his grandfather had won."

Ellen tilted her head. "Disappeared?" she said.

Joe nodded. Then he told her the rest of the story. He spoke about the sneaker prints he had seen outside Timmy's basement window, and about what Travis had told him at Oakdale Sports & Games, and finally about his visit to Damont's house.

"And guess what?" said Joe. "We found the trophy in Damont's garage. But he insisted he hadn't stolen it. He said someone else had put the trophy in his garage to make him look bad."

Ellen sat back in her chair. "Wow!" she said.

"He even had an idea who it might be," Joe added.

He told his mother about how he had confronted Wade in school, and how the boy had denied stealing the trophy. Then he told her about the antiques store and the idea he'd had.

"It sounds like a good idea to me," his mom said. "But I'd hate to think Damont or Wade would do something as bad as stealing."

Joe nodded. "Me, too."

After he finished cleaning up his breakfast dishes, he gave his mother a kiss on the cheek, then headed out the door. As always, Wishbone was right behind him.

Wishbone let Joe take the lead until they got to the sidewalk. Then he couldn't contain himself anymore.

He scampered up ahead, feeling the roughness of the sidewalk underneath his paws. As he ran, he resisted the urge to chase a chipmunk hiding in the bushes near their house.

"Sorry," he told the chipmunk. "Maybe another time. Right now, I've got places to go and people to see."

The chipmunk wasn't the only distraction Wishbone would have to ignore on his way to the antiques store. He also had to pass up a couple of squirrels, a bird, a brand-new tennis ball, and some freshly overturned earth.

"So many opportunities for adventure, so little time," Wishbone said.

Of course, searching the antiques store would be an adventure, too, in a way. But with any luck, it would be more than that. It would be a chance for Wishbone to help Joe—and Sparky, too.

Little by little, Wishbone and Joe made their way to the center of Oakdale. They passed some of the places the terrier had gone by the other day, when he was trailing the Brute.

They went by Beck's Grocery, which was already quite busy this early in the morning. They also walked by Pepper Pete's, which didn't do any breakfast business, and therefore hadn't opened yet.

Next, they passed the First Commerce Bank of Oakdale, with its tall, stately columns. Finally, they came within sight of Oakdale Attic Antiques. Even from a distance, Wishbone could see that the antiques shop was open for business.

That was good, because Wishbone had some business of his own to carry out there. *Detective* business. His tail was already wagging furiously in anticipation of what he might find.

Joe told Wishbone to wait outside. He then opened the door and went inside. Just before the door closed, Wishbone scurried in behind him, though Joe didn't notice.

At that early hour, with the sun still low in the sky, the antiques store had an almost misty look to it. It was as if the store were a forest and every antique in it was some strange-looking variety of tree.

And there were certainly plenty of antiques there—a lot more than Wishbone had seen in Timmy's basement. In fact, there were a lot more than he had seen anywhere in his whole life.

There were wicker tables and delicate-looking dishes, old-fashioned radios and rubber hand puppets, rocking chairs and eyeglasses and ladies' hats. There were lumpy baseball gloves and

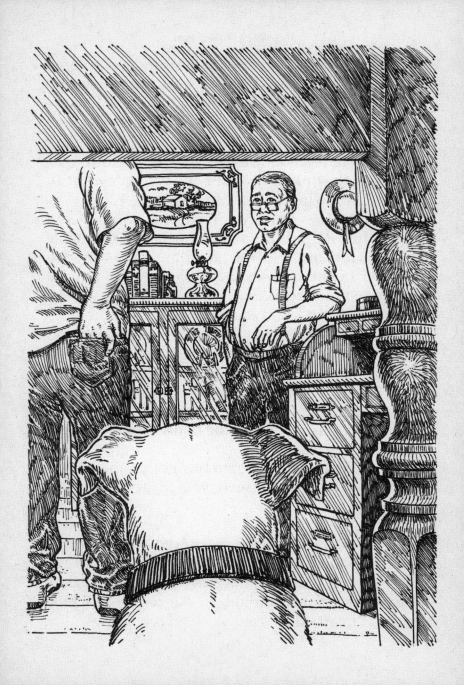

framed tapestries, heavy bronze lamps and colored bottles, leatherbound books and fancy jewelry, and even a big, stuffed parrot.

It was an odd collection, all right. But, in a funny way, it all seemed to fit together, as if everything in the store felt comfortable with everything else. That was the only way Wishbone could describe it.

"Can I help you?" asked a voice.

Wishbone followed it to its source—and found himself peering through the legs of a table at Mr. Hubbard. He was standing by a wooden counter in the back of the place, next to an old-fashioned cash register.

"I hope so," said Joe.

He made his way toward the back of the store. So did Wishbone, his eyes and ears and nose on the alert.

The Brute's thick, musky scent was in the store, all right. However, the smell was pretty faint. Obviously, the big dog hadn't spent a whole lot of time there.

Suddenly, Mr. Hubbard recognized Joe. "Why, hello, son. I haven't seen you in a while, now, have I?"

"No, sir," said Joe.

Mr. Hubbard's eyes narrowed as he caught sight of Wishbone. "Hang on a second," said the shopkeeper. "We can't have any pets in here, son." He shrugged his shoulders. "Too many fragile items, I'm afraid."

Joe was surprised to see Wishbone standing there. "Where did you come from?" he asked. "I thought I left you outside."

"Gosh!" said Wishbone. "This is the second time I'm getting kicked out of this place. I'm starting to get a complex."

Joe knelt in front of him. "Sorry, boy," he said, "but I'll be right out. What I've got to do won't take long."

The shopkeeper smiled sympathetically. "I know it's not easy to ask an animal to sit outside. I'm dog-sitting for my brother's pooch while he's away on vacation, and he doesn't like it, either. Fortunately, I've got a storage shed out back where he can lounge to his heart's content."

"Pooch?" said Wishbone. "Storage shed?"

That was all he needed to know with regard to Sparky's chew-toy problem—and he was eager to turn that knowledge into action. But he didn't like the idea of leaving Joe to pursue his trophy mystery on his own.

After all, Wishbone was the master detective around there. Joe was just starting out.

The boy looked at him. "Come on, Wishbone. You heard Mr. Hubbard. You've got to leave."

With no other choice, the terrier did an about-face and padded over to the front door of the antiques store. Then he looked back at Joe.

Mr. Hubbard chuckled. "How about that? Now there's a pooch who doesn't mind obeying the rules."

Joe grunted. "I guess not."

The boy followed Wishbone to the door. Then he opened it and let him out. "See you in a minute," Joe told him.

"Right," said the terrier.

But he had no intention of leaving the area— at least, not until he heard the outcome of Joe's investigation.

As the door closed again, Wishbone planted himself on the hard cement walk outside and put his superior sense of hearing to work. If he concentrated really hard, he could hear Joe's footsteps on the shop's hardwood floor.

And if I can hear that, he thought, *it'll be a cinch to listen in on Joe's conversation with Mr. Hubbard.*

Chapter Nine

When Joe returned to the back of the store, Mr. Hubbard was waiting for him. "Now, then," said the shopkeeper, "what type of item are you in the market for? A gift for your mother, perhaps?"

Joe blushed. "I'm not exactly in the market for anything, really. I just have a . . . well, a question."

Mr. Hubbard peered at him over his glasses. "A question, you say? Well, I'll certainly answer it if I can."

Joe cleared his throat. "You see, I have this friend, and . . . and I think he might have stolen something from one of my other friends."

The man's brow creased. "Stolen something? Really?"

Joe nodded. "It was an antique, too. That's the reason I'm here. I thought my friend might have come in here to try to sell the thing he stole—I mean, the thing I *think* he stole."

"I understand what you're saying," the shop-keeper assured Joe.

Mr. Hubbard bit his lip as he gave the matter some thought. After a moment or two, he shook his head.

"Nope," he said. "Can't say any kids have come in here trying to sell me anything. In fact, it's been a couple of weeks since *anyone* tried to sell me anything, youngster or adult."

"I see," said Joe.

In a way, he was disappointed. After all, he had hoped to wrap up his case on the basis of what the shopkeeper would tell him, but now it seemed he couldn't do that.

In another way, however, Joe was relieved. If Damont hadn't come into the shop to try to sell the trophy, there was still a chance he was innocent—still a possibility he was telling the truth.

"Thanks," Joe added. "I appreciate your help."

Mr. Hubbard smiled. "I just wish I could've been *more* helpful."

"You've been *very* helpful," the boy assured him. "In fact—"

Suddenly, Joe caught sight of something—something sitting in the back of the store, in an open trunk.

He swallowed. Hard.

"Son?" said the shopkeeper, leaning forward. "Are you all right?"

A smile broke out on Joe's face. "I'm fine," he

managed to say. "Er . . . do you mind if I ask you another question?"

"Not at all," said Mr. Hubbard.

"It's about that trunk," the boy explained.

The shopkeeper seemed confused for a moment. "Trunk?" he said.

Joe pointed to it. "The one behind you."

Mr. Hubbard turned and noticed the trunk in question. "Oh," he said. "*That* trunk." He turned back to Joe. "So what's your question?"

Joe told him.

A few minutes later, the boy had all the information he needed to solve the mystery. At long last, he knew what had happened to Timmy's grandfather's trophy.

But it wasn't enough that *he* knew. Joe had to share what he had learned with everyone else.

He looked directly at Mr. Hubbard. "Sir, would it be possible to *borrow* the trunk? Just for a little while?"

The man stroked his chin. "I don't get too many requests to borrow things, son. My business is selling them."

"It's for a good cause," Joe said. Then he did his best to explain what he meant.

When he was done, Mr. Hubbard sighed. "Well," he said, "this isn't the sort of thing I usually do, but . . . well, you and your mom are good customers. I'll lend you the trunk and the things inside it. Except . . ."

"Yes?" said Joe.

"I'll need to speak with your mother. I want a guarantee from her that I'll get everything back in one piece."

Joe smiled. "I think I can arrange that."

"Good," said Mr. Hubbard. "Then you've got a deal, son." He held his hand out for Joe to shake.

The boy shook it. "Thanks, sir. You won't regret this."

Wishbone did a backflip on the sidewalk outside the antiques store. "Way to go, Joe!" he said excitedly.

The boy had tracked down his thief. Now it was time for the terrier to do the same.

Wishbone went to the narrow alley between the antiques store and the neighboring movie theater. The Brute's scent was there also.

"Well," said Wishbone, "here goes nothing." He started down the alley, not quite certain what he would find at the end of it.

Gradually, the Brute's scent got stronger and stronger . . . and stronger. Obviously, Wishbone realized, he was on the right track.

A little farther along, he caught a glimpse of green ahead and to the right. It seemed there was a yard of some kind there. And if it *was* a yard, it was a likely place for a storage shed.

For all Wishbone knew, the big dog was rolling around in the shed at that very moment, unaware that he would soon have company. Or maybe he was already aware of it, and was licking his chops in anticipation.

Either way, Wishbone wasn't backing off. He had made a promise to himself that he would recover Sparky's chew toys. No matter what obstacles he had to get past, no matter what dangers he had to face, that was exactly what he planned to do.

His senses alert, Wishbone came to the end of the alley and peered around the corner. Sure enough, the piece of green he had glimpsed was part of a tiny, overgrown backyard hidden behind the antiques shop. In the middle of the yard stood a gray-aluminum shed.

The shed's door was open a crack, but it was dark inside—too dark to make out its contents. Fortunately, Wishbone's nose worked as well in darkness as it did in bright light.

He sniffed the air all around him. Wishbone could still detect the Brute's scent, but his nose told him that the big dog himself wasn't around. In fact, as far as Wishbone could tell, the Brute hadn't been there for hours.

For him, that was good news. In fact, that was *very* good news. "When the Brute's away, the detective will play."

Cautiously, Wishbone slipped into the shed, his tail wagging in anticipation of what he might find there. At first, all he saw was a blanket and a couple of dishes. One dish was half full of water. The other had a few crumbs of dog food in it.

Wishbone sniffed it—and turned his nose up. "Not my brand," he said. "I only dine on the good stuff."

Then he saw a pile in the corner of the shed. Padding over to it, Wishbone realized he had struck pay dirt. Mixed in with a couple of chewed-up tennis balls and plastic bottles were two rawhide chew toys.

Sparky's chew toys.

Unfortunately, the golden retriever's football had been mangled almost beyond recognition, just like the fake bone in Sparky's backyard. Wishbone nudged the football aside with his nose. There was no longer any point in bringing it back to its rightful owner.

But fate had been kinder to Sparky's pretzel. As far as Wishbone could tell, it was still in terrific shape.

The terrier picked up the chew toy in his mouth, but he didn't get a very good grip on it. Certainly, it wasn't a good enough grip to bring the pretzel all the way back to Sparky's house. Putting the toy down again, he got his teeth all the way around it.

There, Wishbone thought. *That's better.*

He tried to picture the look of gratitude on his friend's face when the rawhide pretzel was returned to him. *I know, I know,* Wishbone thought, *I'm your hero—and deservedly so.*

With that happy notion in mind, he slipped out of the shed. But before he could get very far, he heard something in the alleyway—something that sounded a lot like a dog's nails scratching the cement.

Uh-oh, he thought.

Wishbone looked around and around for an escape route, but there wasn't any. The fence around the little yard was too high for him to leap over it. With no other option, he turned and stood his ground.

The shadow of something big spilled into the small yard. A moment later, Wishbone caught the thing's scent.

He gulped. The Brute was home.

And the big dog was none too happy, if the growls coming from his throat were any sign. Apparently, the Brute had detected Wishbone's scent, just as Wishbone had detected his.

Okay, Wishbone told himself. *You know the drill. Just stay calm and show him you're not afraid. That's the way to deal with a bully.*

At least, that was what he had always heard.

A moment later, the Brute jogged into view. The look in his spooky, pale eyes wasn't a pleasant one. After all, Wishbone had invaded the big dog's privacy, even if it was for the best of reasons.

The Brute lowered his head between his

two powerful shoulders and pulled his lips back, exposing long, sharp teeth. His eyes turned red-rimmed with fury. With a dangerous sound coming from the depths of his throat, he advanced on the terrier.

Wishbone didn't move a muscle. He just stood there, matching the big dog glare for glare and snarl for snarl.

"Nice teeth you've got there," the terrier said. "But let me tell you as a friend, you really ought to floss more."

No doubt, the Brute had expected Wishbone to drop the chew toy and scamper away. When he didn't, it seemed to confuse the big dog. He stopped in mid-growl and eyed Wishbone, wondering what to do next.

You see? Wishbone thought. *It works every time. Just stand up to a bully and he'll see you're not a pushover.*

He was still thinking that when the Brute barked and launched his powerful body at Wishbone. Yelping despite the toy in his mouth, the terrier skittered out of the way just in time.

Well, maybe it doesn't always *work,* he thought.

Turning instantly, the Brute bunched his muscles and hurtled toward Wishbone a second time. Again, the terrier escaped injury—but only by the narrowest of margins.

"This is definitely not going according to plan," he said.

Wishbone had to do something—and quickly. Otherwise, Sparky would never see his toy *or* his friend again. But what could Wishbone do? The Brute was bigger, stronger and meaner than he was.

And a whole lot angrier.

Wait a minute, Wishbone thought. *If he's that angry, he isn't thinking straight. He's just charging blindly.*

The terrier, on the other hand, was calm, cool, and collected—when he wasn't leaping out of the way of the big dog's teeth and paws.

Suddenly, Wishbone got an idea. As the Brute skidded to a halt and turned on him again, the terrier took up a position right in front of the aluminum storage shed.

Any level-headed canine would have seen through Wishbone's strategy. But at the moment, the big dog was far from level-headed. He was so caught up in his anger that all he could see was his target.

With a growl, the Brute leaped in Wishbone's direction. The terrier waited until the last possible moment—then dashed for safety as fast as his four legs could carry him.

For a fraction of a second, he was afraid he had waited too long. He could feel the big dog's hot breath on his face. He could even smell what the Brute had had for breakfast.

But by the time the big dog's jaw snapped shut, Wishbone was gone. Unfortunately for the Brute, that meant there was nothing to stop his headlong rush—and with a sound like thunder, he smashed into the side of the shed at top speed.

As Wishbone turned to look back at his opponent, he saw the Brute had been stunned by his collision with the shed.

Then he saw the big dog begin to stir. Suddenly, Wishbone's only thought was to get out of the little yard while he still could.

"Exit, stage left," he said.

Then he took off like a shot. His legs pumping, he ran from one end of the alley to the other in record time.

Before he knew it, Wishbone was out of the

alley and back on the sidewalk in front of the antiques store. As luck would have it, Joe was there, too. The boy looked at him wonderingly.

"Where have you been? Are you okay?" he asked.

"Don't ask," Wishbone told him.

Joe took a closer look. "Say . . . that's not one of *your* chew toys, is it?"

Wishbone allowed himself a glance back toward the alleyway. There was no hint of the big dog there, at least for the time being. But, of course, that situation could change—and change quickly.

"Er . . . shouldn't we be going?" he suggested to his pal. "I mean, there's no place like home. Isn't that what they say?"

Right on cue, a familiar Ford Explorer pulled up—with an equally familiar face at the wheel. Smiling, Joe's mom unlocked the doors.

Wishbone didn't hesitate. As soon as Joe opened the door just a crack, the terrier leaped inside and gratefully took a seat next to Ellen.

"No sense in taking unnecessary chances," he said, "especially when the necessary ones are so fur-raising."

Joe's mom looked at him. "Wishbone," she said, "that's not *your* chew toy . . . is it?"

"Like I said before," Wishbone told her, "don't ask."

Remembering why she was there, Ellen turned

to Joe. "Do you need help with the trunk?" she asked.

For the first time, Wishbone noticed the black trunk standing on the sidewalk next to Joe. The boy waved away the suggestion.

"I can handle it," he assured his mother.

And handle it he did. Grabbing the trunk with both hands, Joe lifted it and carried it to the back of the Explorer. Then he set it down on the asphalt. When Ellen popped the lock, the boy opened the door, hefted the trunk again, and slid it inside. Finally, he closed the door.

"Ready to roll," Joe told his mom.

"So am I," Wishbone chimed in, keeping a wary eye on the alley.

But by the time Joe opened the passenger's-side door and got in next to his pal, the big dog still hadn't shown up. *Maybe he's learned the error of his ways, after all,* Wishbone thought.

A moment later, Ellen pulled away from the curb. The terrier readjusted his grip on the rawhide pretzel with a great deal of satisfaction. After all, he had done what he had set out to do—he had recovered Sparky's toy.

"Mission accomplished," he said.

Ellen glanced at Joe. "So," she said, "is that trunk really as important as you said it was on the phone?"

The boy nodded solemnly. "Right now, Mom, it's *very* important."

And he went on to tell her about it.

Of course, Wishbone already knew the meaning of the black trunk, thanks to his eavesdropping outside the antiques store. Wagging his tail happily, he updated his earlier comment.

"Make that *two* missions accomplished."

Chapter Ten

It was still early on Saturday morning when Wishbone got home. As soon as Joe opened the door, the terrier jumped out of the Explorer.

"You know," he told Joe, "you're going to need time to drag the trunk into the house and plan your next step. Why don't I zip over to Sparky's for a minute and give him his chew toy?"

Joe didn't seem to have any objections. He was too busy lugging the trunk out of the back of the Explorer.

"Great," said Wishbone. He took off eagerly in the direction of Sparky's backyard.

With all four of his legs churning up a storm, it didn't take him long to get there. Sparky was sitting in his usual place, in front of his doghouse. At the sight of Wishbone, he began to wag his tail. And when he saw what was in the terrier's mouth, he wagged even harder.

"You don't need to say anything," Wishbone told Sparky. "I mean it. The look on your face is thanks enough."

Then he dropped the rawhide pretzel at his friend's paws.

Sparky's tail wagged as fast as Wishbone had ever seen a tail wag. Filled with delight, the golden retriever picked up the toy in his mouth and ran all around the yard with it.

"Hey," said Wishbone, spinning in place to watch, "slow down, all right? You're making me dizzy."

Then he got a whiff of something. Something *bad*.

Turning his head, Wishbone saw the Brute make his way into the yard. The terrier's first thought was to warn Sparky—to let him know they might have a fight on their paws.

Then he saw that the big dog was clutching something in his mouth. It was a tennis ball—one of the items Wishbone had seen inside the Brute's shed.

By then, Sparky had noticed the big dog, too, and stopped in front of his doghouse. Without even a hint of a grudge, the Brute padded over to Wishbone and put the tennis ball down in front of him.

Wishbone had been a dog long enough to understand what that meant. The big dog was making a peace offering. He wanted to be the terrier's *friend*.

Wishbone wagged his tail. "Well," he said happily—and not without a certain amount of relief—"that's a dog of a different color."

Apparently, he had earned the Brute's respect by standing up to him in back of the antiques store.

"I get it," said Wishbone. "Anyone who could knock you out has to be worth knowing better?"

The Brute didn't say anything. He just wagged his tail.

Wishbone took that for a "yes."

"So," he said to the big dog, "want to catch falling leaves?"

He wasn't sure who seemed more enthusiastic about it—the Brute or Sparky.

119

The next day was Sunday.

Joe stood by the door of his porch and watched his friend David approach from the driveway. He took a deep breath and opened the door.

"Here we go, boy," said Joe. "Wish me luck."

Wishbone, who was sitting beside him, snuffled and wagged his tail. He seemed as excited as Joe himself.

"Hi," said David.

"Hi," Joe replied.

"What's up?" asked David.

"You'll see," said Joe. "Come on inside."

As David joined him on the porch, Joe could already see Sam coming around the house. The other kids couldn't be far behind, he thought.

"Hi, Joe," said Sam as she got a bit closer. She grinned. "So what's the big mystery?"

"All will be revealed in good time," Joe replied, echoing a line he had once heard in a movie.

After all, he didn't want to give anything away until he was ready, and he wouldn't be ready until the rest of his guests had arrived.

He had read more of *Peril at End House* the night before. And that was how Hercule Poirot had handled the situation. He had gathered all his suspects together, so he could tell everyone at once the identity of the person who had killed Nick Buckley's cousin Maggie.

If it was good enough for Poirot, Joe thought, it was good enough for him, too.

As Sam walked in, she saw David standing beside Joe. She looked at Joe questioningly, then turned to David.

"What do *you* know about this?" she asked him.

David shrugged. "Not much. In fact, nothing at all. Old tight-lips there asked me to come over, but he wouldn't say why."

Sam nodded. "Same here."

"Just bear with me a while," Joe said. "Believe me, neither one of you will be sorry."

Just then, Timmy showed up at the door. Sam opened it and let the new kid in.

"Samantha?" asked Timmy.

"In the flesh," she replied.

Timmy seemed surprised that she and David were there. He looked at Joe. "I thought you wanted to talk to me," he said.

"I do," Joe told him. "In fact, I want to talk to all of you."

"All three of us?" asked David.

"All *four* of us," Sam responded.

She jerked her head in the direction of the door, where Damont had just made an appearance. As the prime suspect let himself in, he looked suspiciously at Joe, then at the others.

"How about that?" he said. "The gang's all here." He looked at Joe again. "And here I thought it was going to be a *private* party."

"I didn't say that," Joe told him.

"You didn't say it wasn't," Damont countered.

"So why *did* you ask us over?" Timmy inquired.

"I'll let you know," Joe responded, "as soon as we're all present and accounted for."

"You mean we're still waiting for someone?" asked Sam.

Out of the corner of Joe's eye, he saw another of his friends coming from the direction of the driveway. "That's right," he said. "And here he is."

A moment later, Wade showed his face. He didn't look at all happy to be there. And when the boy saw who was waiting for him, his mood didn't improve one bit.

"What's going on?" he asked, his voice cold and unfriendly.

Joe wasn't surprised at Wade's attitude. If he himself had been accused of stealing, he probably wouldn't have been in a real good mood, either.

"That's a good question," said Damont.

David, Sam, and Timmy didn't say a thing. They just looked at Joe, waiting for an explanation.

"Why don't we all go into the kitchen and have a seat?" Joe suggested.

One by one, the kids moved into the next room and pulled up chairs. First David. Then Samantha. Then Timmy and Damont. And finally, Wade.

Wishbone curled up in a corner of the room. However, his tail was still wagging as hard as before.

Joe cleared his throat. "First," he said, "I want to thank everybody for coming over."

"I didn't mind coming," said Timmy. "But now that we're here, can you tell us *why?*"

"Yeah," said Damont. "What's the big mystery? Or are you going to blame me for something *else* I didn't do?"

David rolled his eyes. "Keep denying it, Damont. Maybe if you do it long enough, someone will believe you."

"Actually," said Joe, "*I* believe him."

David looked at his friend. "You do?"

Joe nodded. "Damont's innocent—and I can prove it."

Wade folded his arms across his chest. "This I've got to see."

Sam looked at Joe. "Me, too," she said.

Of course, she didn't sound skeptical, the way David and Wade did. She sounded hopeful that Joe would get Damont off the hook.

"You see," Joe began, "deep down inside, I was never really convinced that Damont was guilty."

"Thank you very much," said Damont. "That's the first reasonable thing I've heard you say in days."

"Unfortunately," Joe went on, "all the evidence seemed to point to Damont. First the sneaker prints, then the trophy being found in his garage. It looked pretty bad for him. And yet, Damont seemed sincere when he told me he thought he'd been framed."

"I *was,*" Damont noted.

Joe ignored him. "At the time," he said, "Damont thought Wade might have been the one who framed him, because he saw Wade on his block. So I talked to Wade about it at school the next day."

Wade didn't say anything, but his eyes had narrowed and he had thrust his hands into his pockets. He looked as if he were daring Joe to make an accusation against him.

"Of course," said Joe, "Wade didn't offer any explanation for being on Damont's block. But that didn't really mean anything. I still couldn't prove someone other than Damont had stolen the trophy."

"That's why you came back to my house," Timmy commented. "To check out the sneaker prints again."

"That's right," said Joe. "But it didn't help. I still couldn't find any evidence that pointed to someone besides Damont."

"And then?" David prodded.

Joe looked at him. "Then Wishbone came home with a business card in his mouth—a card that happened to be from Oakdale Attic Antiques. When I saw it, I got an idea. I mean, if Damont had stolen the trophy to sell it, who would he try to sell it *to?*"

David snapped his fingers. "An antiques store—of course!"

"Exactly," said Joe. "So I went there to ask Mr. Hubbard if he'd gotten any offers from Damont."

"Which he hadn't," Damont pointed out.

"True," Joe replied. "But my visit wasn't a

complete waste of time. While I was at the store, I noticed something interesting."

The boy left his friends then and went into the next room, where he had placed the black trunk he'd gotten from the antiques store. Bending his knees and getting a good grip on it, he hefted the trunk and carried it into the kitchen.

"What's that?" asked Wade, his features puckering with curiosity.

"An old trunk?" said Samantha.

"What's that got to do with anything?" asked David.

"Yeah," said Damont. "What's the scoop?"

Joe patted the trunk. "Believe it or not, the answer to the mystery of who took the trophy is right here."

"Go ahead, open it, Joe," David told him.

Joe did exactly that. He lifted the lid of the trunk and showed everyone its contents. The kids all came closer to get a better view.

"Wow!" said Sam.

"I'll say," David added.

There were a half-dozen bronze trophies inside the trunk. They looked old, too—as old as the trophy Timmy's grandfather had won. Wishbone approached them and sniffed around a bit.

Sam reached into the trunk and picked up one of the trophies. She read the plaque on its base: "'Kingsport Cougars, Appalachian League Champions, 1943. Tyrone Randall, Forward.'"

"Hey," said David, as Sam put the trophy back in the trunk, "that guy played on the same team with Timmy's grandfather."

Wade picked up a trophy and checked its plaque. "This one went to Samuel Hayes, another guard." He took out another trophy and held it in his other hand. "And this one was for Davis-Rhodes, the center."

Joe nodded. "Each plaque is made out to someone different. But all of these trophies were given to the Appalachian League champions in the year 1943—just like the one we saw in Timmy's basement. The more I thought about it, the more it seemed to me that was a pretty big coincidence."

"That's right," Damont piped up. "It *is.*"

"So," said Joe, "I asked Mr. Hubbard about it. He told me he had sold one of the trophies—along with a bunch of other antiques—to a new family in town. I asked him if he could remember their name. He said he couldn't, but he could look it up in his files."

Joe looked at Timmy. In fact, by then, *everyone* was looking at Timmy. The boy seemed to grow pale under their scrutiny.

"Their last name was Ashbury," Joe said. "Just like Timmy's."

"What are you saying?" asked David.

Joe glanced at him. "Remember that antique dealer's card that Timmy showed us? It wasn't in his basement because Mr. Hubbard wanted to *buy* Timmy's family's antiques. It was there because

Oakdale Attic Antiques had *sold* some of that stuff to Timmy's mom and dad."

David looked at Joe, then at Timmy, then at Joe again. "So . . . Timmy lied to us about the card?"

"That's ridiculous," said Timmy.

But Joe was sure of what he was saying. "Timmy lied about the card—and about the trophy, too. It didn't belong to his grandfather after all. It was just something cool-looking his mom and dad had bought at the antiques store."

"But that doesn't explain who took it," Samantha pointed out.

"You're right," said Joe. "It doesn't. But once I realized Timmy wasn't telling the truth about the card or the trophy, I wondered if he had lied to us about other things—for instance, whether the trophy had even been stolen in the first place."

Wade looked at him. "You think . . . ?"

"I think Timmy lied about the trophy being stolen," Joe said, completing his friend's thought for him. "I think he made those sneaker prints himself. And I think he planted the trophy in Damont's garage so we would find it there and think Damont took it."

Timmy got angry. "That's a lie!" he declared.

Damont looked squinty-eyed at him. "So Timmy wasn't the injured party after all. He was the guilty one."

That's right, Joe thought. *Just like in* Peril at End House, *where the apparent victim, Nick Buckley, turned out to be the murderer.*

"Then that's the answer to the mystery?" David asked. "It was *Timmy* who took the trophy out of his own basement?"

Joe looked at the new boy. "That's right," he said. "It was Timmy who stole the trophy."

Chapter Eleven

"'Attaboy, Joe!" Wishbone crowed. "Spoken like a true detective."

Just like Hercule Poirot, in fact. After all, Poirot had come to the same conclusion in *Peril at End House*—that a "victim" who lied about *one* thing had probably lied about everything else as well.

In Poirot's case, the one who lied had been Nick Buckley. She had told the detective she sent for her cousin Maggie at his suggestion—when, in truth, she had sent for Maggie earlier than that.

Once Poirot began to distrust Nick, he put two and two together—realizing that Cousin Maggie's name was really Magdala as well. Right from the beginning, it had all been a plot on Nick's part to kill her cousin and inherit the fortune left to the other "Magdala Buckley."

"Only one unfinished item still remains," said Wishbone.

In every good "whodunit," the guilty party spoke up in the end—even if it was just to deny the charges made against him. Wishbone looked to Timmy for his reaction to Joe's accusation.

Suddenly, the boy leaped to his feet. "I thought you were my friend!" he screamed at Joe. "Why are you doing this to me? Why are you making everyone hate me?"

Before Joe or anyone else could answer him, Timmy bolted from the room and ran out the back door of the house.

"Somebody should get him," said Samantha.

Wishbone agreed.

He slipped out the door before Timmy could slam it shut. Then he sped down the driveway, overtook the fleeing boy, and barked at him.

"Leave me alone!" Timmy shouted at the terrier.

But Wishbone knew the boy would regret it if he left. "When somebody does something wrong," Wishbone said, "they've got to face the consequences. Otherwise, it'll haunt them the rest of their life."

Maybe he was being a little too dramatic, but what he was saying was certainly the truth.

"I said leave me alone!" Timmy shouted a little louder.

"No," said a voice. "Wishbone was right to stop you."

The terrier looked up and saw that Samantha had caught up with Timmy, too. She looked almost as hurt as Timmy was.

"Please," she said. "Don't run away, Timmy. Running never solves anything."

"That's exactly what I was telling him," Wishbone pointed out.

Timmy looked at Sam, his face red with embarrassment, his eyes hard and angry. Then he looked back at Joe's house, where the other kids were sticking their heads out the front door to see what would happen.

"I can't go back in there," he whispered.

"You have to," Sam insisted. "Trust me, okay?"

For a moment, Wishbone wasn't sure they were going to get through to the kid. Then Timmy swallowed hard, turned around and started back to the house.

When the other kids saw him coming, they stuck their heads back inside. Soon, they were all gathered in the kitchen again—Wishbone, Samantha and Timmy included.

Everybody was quiet at first. Then David spoke up.

"I don't get it," he said. "Why would you want to pretend the trophy was your grand-father's—and then tell us someone had stolen it?"

Joe turned to Timmy. "That's the one part I haven't been able to figure out."

Everyone waited for Timmy to respond to Joe's statement. Finally, Timmy took a deep breath.

"All right," he said softly, looking down at the floor. "I admit it. The trophy never belonged to my grandfather. It wasn't stolen. And I was the one who took it and put it in Damont's garage."

"But what for?" asked Wishbone.

Timmy shrugged, as if in response to the terrier's question. "I guess I . . . I wanted to . . ." He sat there for a moment. "I mean, I was only . . ."

Wishbone could see that Timmy was having a hard time of it. He wished he could make it easier somehow on the boy. But of course, he couldn't.

Fortunately, there was someone who *could*. She had been standing in the next room, though no one except Joe and Wishbone had been aware of it until that very moment.

A pretty woman with a reddish-blond ponytail walked into the kitchen, followed closely by Joe's mom. "I think I can explain," the woman said.

Damont looked at her. "Er . . . who are you?"

The woman frowned ever so slightly. "I'm Timmy's mother."

Timmy's eyes were as big as golf balls. "Mom?" he said, stunned. "What are *you* doing here?"

"Joe's mother told me about the missing trophy," Mrs. Ashbury explained. "She asked me to come over and hear what Joe had to say." She glanced sadly at Ellen. "Now I'm glad she did."

Timmy turned away. He seemed terribly ashamed of himself.

His mother looked at the other kids. "I guess Timmy and I owe you all an apology. I wish I could tell you this was the first time he had done something like this. Unfortunately, it isn't."

"It isn't?" Sam replied.

Mrs. Ashbury sighed. "You see," she said, "Timmy's father has the kind of job that forces us to move a lot from place to place. Timmy's had to make new friends each time, and sometimes that can be a difficult task."

"Isn't that the truth," Wishbone said.

"But," said Timmy's mother, "Timmy's found that if he can impress kids with his family's achievements, or make them feel bad for him . . . or just get them interested in a mystery that revolves around him, he can make friends a little more easily."

"And if he can do all three of those things," Wishbone figured, "things are likely to go even better for him."

Timmy's scheme worked pretty well, too, Wishbone realized—that was, until Joe finally dug deep enough to see through it.

Mrs. Ashbury sighed again. "We had hoped Timmy was through with this kind of behavior. I see we still have a lot of work ahead of us."

Timmy was silent. He obviously didn't know what to say.

"But why pick on *me?*" Damont asked suddenly. "Why did you try to make me look like the bad guy? Didn't you think about what it would do to my reputation?"

Wishbone snorted. "Some reputation," he said.

"Sorry," said Timmy, looking sheepishly at Damont. "I didn't mean to hurt you. Not really."

"So why did you?" Damont demanded.

Timmy frowned. "I was angry at you," he said. "I didn't like the things you did to me on the basketball court." He glanced at his mother. "But I was wrong—I know that now. Whatever

Damont did to me, it wasn't half as bad as what I did to *him*."

Timmy looked at Joe, then Samantha, and finally at David.

"I guess you'll never want to be my friends now," he said sadly.

Joe shrugged. "I don't know. You pulled a dirty trick, all right. But I think everyone deserves a break."

Ellen smiled at Joe. Obviously, she was proud of him. So was Wishbone. They had done a good job of raising the boy.

David nodded. "A break. I'll go along with that."

"Me, too," said Sam. She looked at Damont. "How about you?"

The Damonster didn't say anything.

"Damont?" Sam said.

Finally, he shrugged. "Yeah, sure . . . why not?"

"I have just one question," Joe told Timmy.

"What's that?" Timmy replied.

"Where did you get a pair of sneakers that matched Damont's?"

Timmy smiled. "It wasn't easy," he admitted. "I had to search a couple of malls before I found them."

His mother seemed surprised. "*That's* why we had to look all afternoon for those sneakers? If I had known . . ."

136

"Listen," said Ellen, "I've got a trunk full of trophies to return to the antiques store."

"I'll give you a hand," said Mrs. Ashbury.

"Me, too," said Timmy. He looked around. "I mean, it's the least I can do after all the trouble I caused."

"If I can make a suggestion," said Joe's mom, "I think your services may be needed elsewhere."

Timmy looked at her. "Where's that?"

"Well," said Ellen, "it's such a nice fall day and all, I'll bet Joe and his friends are going to want to play basketball. And as I understand it, it's not easy to get enough kids for two teams."

Timmy smiled at her. Then he looked at Joe. "What do you think?" Timmy asked hopefully.

Joe shrugged. "Sounds good to me."

"I'll second that motion," said David.

"Me, too," said Wade.

"Count me in," said Sam.

Damont looked at the others and scowled. Finally, he said, "Hey, why not? But this time, no one's escaping because of a little rain."

Wishbone approved. "As Shakespeare once said, all's well that ends well. And it looks like this is ending pretty well, considering how badly things started out."

"Come on," said Joe. "I'll get my ball."

But before he could go anywhere, Wishbone grabbed his pal's pants leg in his teeth. Then, when Joe knelt to pet him, he licked Joe's face.

"Hey," said the boy, "what's that for?"

"You know," Wishbone told his pal, "you're a terrific detective, Joe. I mean, a really terrific detective. I mean, a really, *really* terrific detective—and a good kid, besides!"

But then, Wishbone thought, that hadn't really come as a surprise to him. After all, the boy had learned at the paws of a master.

About Michael Jan Friedman

Michael Jan Friedman is a *New York Times* best-selling author. He has written or co-written thirty science fiction, fantasy, and young-adult novels. More than 4 million of his books are currently in print in the United States alone.

Friedman had an especially good time writing *The Stolen Trophy*. He's always been fascinated by mysteries, and those of Agatha Christie are among his favorites.

Friedman has also been a fan and collector of antiques for a long time. He believes that antiques are mysteries, too, in a way. From his point of view, each antique represents something that happened in the life of a human being—something hidden by time. It's fun to look at an old baseball or painting or rocking chair and try to unlock the mystery by imagining who owned these objects and what these people were like.

Friedman became a freelance writer in 1985, after the publication of his first book, a heroic fantasy called *The Hammer and The Horn*. Since then, he has written for television, radio, magazines, and comic books, though his first love is still the novel.

A native New Yorker, Friedman received his undergraduate degree from the University of

Pennsylvania, and his graduate degree from Syracuse University's Newhouse School. He lives with his wife and children on Long Island, where he spends his free time sailing on Long Island Sound, jogging, and following his favorite baseball team, the New York Yankees.

Appear in a WISHBONE™ Mystery!

One lucky winner (age seven through twelve) will have the chance to help Wishbone™ solve a mystery by appearing in an upcoming WISHBONE Mysteries book! The winner will have his or her photograph on the front cover of a future book, a role in the story, and his or her likeness in an illustration in the text. Enter today! Simply hand-print your name, address, birthday, and your favorite mystery story of all time on a 3"-by-5" card, or on the official entry blank available at participating retailers. Mail to:

WISHBONE • BIG FEATS! ENTERTAINMENT • ATTN: MYSTERY SERIES SWEEPSTAKES
P.O. BOX 3472 • YOUNG AMERICA, MN 55558-3472

Coming Soon!

The SUPER Adventures of
WISHBONE

#1

Dog Days OF THE WEST

By Vivian Sathre
Inspired by *Heart of the West* by O. Henry

WHAT HAS FOUR LEGS, A HEALTHY COAT, AND A GREAT DEAL ON MEMBERSHIP?

IT'S THE WISHBONE ZONE™
THE OFFICIAL WISHBONE™ FAN CLUB!

When you enter the **WISHBONE ZONE,** you get:
- Color poster of **Wishbone**™
- **Wishbone** newsletter filled with photos, news, and games
- Autographed photo of **Wishbone** and his friends
- **Wishbone** sunglasses, and more!

To join the fan club, pay $10 and charge your **WISHBONE ZONE** membership to VISA, MasterCard, or Discover. Call:

1-800-888-WISH

Or send us your name, address, phone number, birth date, and a check for $10 payable to Big Feats! (TX residents add $.83 sales tax/IN residents add $.50 sales tax). Write to:

WISHBONE ZONE
P.O. Box 9523
Allen, TX 75013-9523

Prices and offer are subject to change. Place your order now!

Now Playing on Your VCR...

Two exciting **Wishbone**® stories on video!

Ready for an adventure? Then leap right in with **Wishbone**™ as he takes you on a thrilling journey through two great action-packed stories. First, there are haunted houses, buried treasure, and mysterious graves in two back-to-back episodes of *A Tail in Twain*, starring **Wishbone** as Tom Sawyer. Then, no one is more powerful than **Wishbone**, in *Hercules* exciting new footage! It's **Wishbone** on Hercules...or rather *Unleashed*, featuring It's more fun than a flea dip! home video.

Available wherever videos are sold.